AN IMPARTIAL EYE

PIERRE BOULLE

Martial Gaur has been an ace war photographer. But a wound in the Algerian War and the resultant artificial leg have blighted his career. Now he is reduced to studio portraits. Then opportunity comes for what can be the greatest *coup* of his career. So obsessed is he with this chance that he can contemplate sacrificing friends, honour, patriotism in order to take it. Will he connive at the assassination of his President in order to get the photograph?

Pierre Boulle

An Impartial Eye

translated from the French by
Xan Fielding

London
Secker & Warburg

First published in France 1967 as
LE PHOTOGRAPHE
by René Julliard, Paris

Copyright © René Julliard 1967

First published in England 1968 by
Martin Secker & Warburg Ltd,
14 Carlisle Street, London W.1

English translation
© Martin Secker & Warburg Ltd 1968

SBN: 436 05808 1

Set in 11 on 13 pt Linotype Times
and printed in Great Britain by
Western Printing Services Ltd, Bristol

Part One

Part One

1

THE STARLET LAY BACK, arching her spine against a cushion on the sofa, the only piece of furniture that might have lent an aspect of luxury to the shabby bed-sitting room. She crossed her legs and thrust out her chest with manifest diligence, as though striving to force the whole of her body out of her scanty clothing. Then she gave the photographer a questioning glance, like an obsequious pupil seeking the approval of his master.

"Like this? Or a little higher?"

He shrugged his shoulders irritably, without replying. She looked anxious and added briskly:

"I can take off my bra, if you like."

Martial Gaur, who for the last few minutes had been observing her through the view-finder with ill-concealed impatience, suddenly lost his temper and flung his camera down on the sofa so violently that she gave a start and shrank back on the cushions.

"Why not your knickers, while you're about it? What do you take me for? Do you think I'm a pornography merchant, or do you consider yourself a real star who can take any liberty she likes?"

"My agent told me . . ."

"Your agent's a bloody fool. Is he taking the pictures or am I? Suggestive pictures, do you hear? Suggestive —didn't anyone ever tell you what that means? Well, it doesn't mean stripping down to the buff."

The girl's lips were pursed into a childish pout. Seeing him advance on her still cursing under his breath, she raised her arm as though to ward off a blow. Martial Gaur's anger was unable to withstand this touching reaction. At once he changed his tone.

"Now you're going to blub! Oh dear! Do pull yourself together, there's a good girl. I'm not a monster. It's just that I know my job, you see, a job I've been doing since long before you were born. Do as I say and you'll have a lovely picture, the loveliest you can imagine, I promise, a picture that will attract millions of admirers, appear in every magazine in the world, and make every producer on both sides of the Atlantic lick his lips. There now. It's the first time you've posed like this, isn't it? Well, then, trust me. Keep a little in reserve for later on. Here, let me fix you."

He hitched up her neckline slightly, made her lower one leg, then stepped back and examined her, wrinkling his brow.

"That's it. But now we'll have to wait till the waterworks are turned off. Blow your nose and make up your face again . . . but don't overdo it. Suggestion is what we're after, remember. You're all the same, you girls."

"I'll do whatever you say."

"You'd better."

She smiled faintly through her tears and sat down at

the end of the room in front of a rickety console which served as a dressing-table. He watched her for a moment, unconsciously ran his finger along a piece of furniture, withdrew it black with dust, shrugged his shoulders again and started pacing to and fro with his hands behind his back, while she kept glancing at him apprehensively. Intimidated now by his silence, she attempted to resume the conversation and, noticing his unsteady gait, enquired:

"Why are you limping? Have you hurt your leg?"

She never failed to put her foot in it! He almost lost his temper again, but controlled himself and merely gave a bitter smile.

"Yes, rather badly. Look."

He hitched up the leg of his trousers and showed her the strip of artificial limb above his sock. She blushed with embarrassment.

"Oh, I'm so sorry. Do forgive me. I didn't know."

"Never mind. Don't start blubbing again, that's all. It happened a long time ago."

"Was it an accident?"

"You could call it that, I suppose. In those days I didn't merely photograph babes like you, my job used to take me to the world's trouble spots."

He lapsed into a gloomy silence again, while she blinked her eyes in front of the mirror. After a moment or two he appeared to wake up.

"Ready? Let's have a look. Yes, that's it. Give us a smile now . . . not like a cow, like a human being, if you can."

She did as she was told. She accepted his gruff and

9

familiar manner without a murmur since it seemed quite natural and contained only a faint touch of contempt, as though he was dealing with a small child or rather an animal, a young animal which he had to train to make it do certain tricks, by forbidding it any undue initiative of its own.

The relationship between them was that of an artist and his subject, a relationship which became even more pronounced during the next stage, when he drew on all the resources of his experience to make her adopt the pose he wanted. He took her by the hand, made her lie down on the sofa, raised her legs himself, marking the limit which was not to be exceeded with an authoritative tap, and succeeded after several attempts in adjusting her neckline to the desired angle. Throughout these preparations his gestures were of an almost maternal gentleness, punctuated by an occasional outburst of impatience when the effect after which he was striving refused to materialise.

This photograph, intended no doubt for some film magazine, was sickeningly banal, granted, but to a real artist there is no such thing as an insignificant subject. Old Tournette, who had taught Martial Gaur all he knew about photography, had brought him up on this precept and still quoted it to him frequently. Gaur had taken it to heart, clinging to it even with a sort of desperate fervour, as though to a religious dogma, now that his disability forced him to confine himself to subjects like this.

Under the judgement of his fastidious eye and the direction of his agile fingers, the starlet played an important part, admittedly, but no more important than the lighting, the sofa and the vase of flowers which she had seen fit to place beside her. Not once did he allow himself to be distracted from the end in view (a satisfactory pose) by the touching and at the same time alluring picture presented by the girl lying half naked on the cushions, flushed from the emotion caused by his recent reprimand, and manifestly submissive to his every wish.

He darted backwards and forwards, wrinkling his brow, his muscles tensed from the constant concern not to neglect a single detail that might contribute to the value of the picture, so immersed in his job as to forget his artificial limb, which made him stumble occasionally on the skimpy carpet. One rebellious thigh gave him a great deal of trouble and imposed a severe strain on his patience. It would not fall into the general picture in a natural manner but obstinately caught every ray of light or else withdrew into the shadows, injecting an incongruous note into the harmony he was striving to create. He spent an infinite time shifting it from one position to another, handling it gently at first, then tugging at it unmercifully, until fresh tears welled up in the girl's eyes. No sooner had he settled this problem than he seized one intractable breast with an exasperated hand and fiercely confined its contours which tended to transgress the rules of strict artistry.

Every so often he would step back from the recumbent body, believing he had found the ideal composition, and rush over to his camera, now fixed on its tripod, as fast as his wretched leg permitted. After observing the result through the view-finder, he would then give a snort of annoyance and return to his subject

11

with the same urgency to rectify some detail which he suddenly considered inadmissible.

"You can talk if you like," he said grumpily, since she was watching his manoeuvres without daring to open her mouth. "It might make you look more natural," he added, clenching his teeth. "Ask me something, anything you like. Go on, don't be frightened. You want to know how I lost my leg, I know."

For the last few minutes he had been exasperated by the lack of expression on her face and was racking his brains to find a subject of interest capable of dispelling her horribly vacant gaze. Believing he had discerned a gleam in her eyes when he had spoken to her about his injury, he decided to make use of this artifice.

"Was your job very dangerous?"

A fresh gleam came into her eyes. She was nibbling at the bait. He endeavoured to exploit this stroke of luck.

"Fairly. I was a photographer, as I am now, but not in the same field."

"A war photographer?"

"You're a sharp little minx, aren't you? I can't keep a thing from you. . . ."

She was now so intrigued as to forget she was the target of his lens: a result at which he always aimed in such circumstances.

"Yes, a war photographer. I've actually been in several wars, if you want to know. This"—he indicated his leg—"this is a souvenir of the last one, in Algeria. . . . That's the expression I wanted. Go on talking. Try and think, do you hear, *think*, I beg you. Now you're beginning to look almost human."

12

He sprang back to his camera and focused it carefully, manipulating various knobs.

"Were you wounded? By a bullet?"

"By several bullets, my beauty, what's known in technical jargon as a burst. The rebels were waiting for us as we landed."

"You were in a plane?"

"Don't open your mouth as though you were yawning. No, not exactly in a plane, we were dropping by parachute.... Good. That's not too bad. Go on talking."

He had taken his first exposure. He pulled a lever and sighted again, his attention focused on a slight accentuation of the curve of her lip which seemed to him full of promise.

"Were there many rebels?"

"No. We had dropped into a ruined hamlet. A more or less pointless operation. There were only three of them. All the rest had taken to their heels."

"Were you a paratrooper?"

Click! This second exposure ought to be good. Her lip was assuming a more and more expressive curve.

"No, a photographer, as I said. But my job obliged me to go into action, sometimes by parachute." Click! "That's fine. Raise your left knee slightly, though. You've gone to the opposite extreme. Now you look like a schoolgirl who's wearing a suspender belt for the first time in her life. Don't stiffen, keep your eyes on me, and never mind the camera.... Yes, there were just three of them left and one of them peppered me in the leg. But I had my revenge. I got him all right."

Click! That gleam in her eye, for which he had been

13

waiting all this time without daring to hope for it unduly, had come and gone in a flash but he was sure he
had caught it. He felt so pleased that he allowed her to
rest for a few minutes.

"Fine. You're a good girl. That's what I wanted.
Try and have a few more inspirations like that. You
can lean on your elbow now if you like."

"You killed him?"

The photographer's face expressed the most ingenuous astonishment.

"Killed him? Me? What for? And what on earth
with? I was unarmed."

"Oh, I don't know . . . You might have done him in
somehow."

Martial burst out laughing.

"While lying on the ground with blood spouting
from my leg, and barely enough strength to hold my
camera? . . . . And miss one of the best pictures of my
career? Don't be silly. I tell you I got him. *I got him*,
you understand? I got him the first time just as he shot
another parachutist dead. I was even lucky enough to
get them both in the same exposure . . . Don't move
now. . . . Then I got him again just as he himself was
shot by one of our fellows. There aren't many of us in
the profession who've had such success with pictures
like that. . . . Not that mine were published all over the
world, but they caused quite a sensation. We were
quits, that rebel and I. . . ." Click! "That's that. You've
been a good girl. You can get up now. I'll send you the
proofs."

14

MARTIAL GAUR struggled down the four flights of stairs in the lodging-house where the starlet lived, cursing the absence of a lift. His artificial leg had never felt so cumbersome and his equipment tugged at his shoulder more than usual.

"Silly little goose!"

He muttered a few other complimentary remarks of this nature under his breath, but without the slightest pejorative intention towards the girl. In fact it was against himself that he was inveighing, against himself and the kind of specialised work which he had been forced to take up since his injury. A pin-up merchant! He who had been one of the most dashing press photographers! The account he had given that girl of one particular episode in his adventurous life tended to unleash a train of melancholy thoughts.

Yet it was not weakness on his part, or the puerile desire to show off, that had made him evoke this past life of his. Martial Gaur was by nature thoroughly immunised against the ignoble lures of weakness and, being rarely moved to pity by the fate of others, was no

15

more moved to pity by his own. As for bragging about his former exploits and glorifying himself, he was far too proud and contemptuous of the opinion of his fellow men in general and women in particular, and above all the sort of silly geese which his profession obliged him to frequent every day. In point of fact, this account was simply a cunning manoeuvre to put the subject in the right mood and bring a lively expression into her eyes. Similarly, his outbursts of temper and uncouth manner did not derive from genuine surliness. It was all thought out and calculated. With some of these girls, with most of them in fact, cursing and swearing yielded results. When that failed, he tried something else. He would have attempted anything (he had occasionally even resorted to physical violence) in order to bring a particular gleam into their eyes.

It so happened that this one had been susceptible to feats of arms (not that she understood a thing about the story of the rebel—she had been fascinated as though by a cheap novelette). Yet thank heavens some useful purpose could still be served by this past of his, which continued to unfold before his eyes in a series of vivid images as he struggled down the dark staircase. The show was over, however. No professional obligation justified these reminiscences which kept flooding back to mind, as had happened frequently for some time. Too frequently: a sure sign of old age. Yet he was only fifty-five and would still have been fighting fit were it not for this damned disability!

With relief he stepped out of the dingy lobby and set off on foot in the direction of the Boulevard Saint-Michel. As he approached it, a vague uproar became

16

audible, recalling him for a brief moment to the realities of the hour. Certain districts in Paris had been in a state of effervescence for several days and the Latin Quarter in particular was steeped in an atmosphere of unrest.

The reason for this commotion was the personage of the President of the Republic, Pierre Malarche, who had been elected a few months before. The traditional right-wing parties reproached the new Head of State for a number of liberal innovations and above all for his relatively young age. He was just over forty, and public feelings, the very feelings no doubt which had formerly rebelled against old age, were now unleashed against youth and inexperience. Since this blemish likewise gave rise, in France, to the instinctive distrust of all the other parties, including those who approved of his policy, young Pierre Malarche had plenty of enemies. Admittedly, he did nothing to appease his opponents and even seemed to take pleasure in provoking them. No sooner had he been elected than he had announced his forthcoming marriage to a film actress years younger even than himself. This taunt had provoked a fresh outburst of indignation and rage among his opponents. Hostile, sometimes violent demonstrations had been taking place every day, orchestrated by some nationalist groups which had lately been reorganised on lines reminiscent of the days of the leagues.

The motives of this unrest seemed utterly futile to Martial Gaur, who for ages had felt nothing but supreme contempt for political affairs. In the old days public disturbances had provided him with the wherewithal for an interesting picture or two but, now that his disability precluded his taking part in a brawl, they merely gave him a fresh excuse for stirring up old memories.

It was actually in a disturbed period like this that his vocation had revealed itself. He looked back at himself as he was in 1936, with no pleasure. He felt nothing but scorn for the silly young fool he then was according to his present-day judgement.

Scarcely had he emerged from childhood than he had abandoned his education more or less completely to embark on politics, or at least what he called politics. This meant taking part in every seditious demonstration, dealing out blows with his fists and occasionally with a cosh, assisted by a few other hotheads, active members like himself of an extreme right-wing league. Which league? He could not even remember exactly, so void of reality did this past life of his appear to him today. His mother was dead and his father, a reactionary journalist, turned a blind eye to his escapades, gave him all the money he wanted and smiled indulgently whenever his son came home with a bump on his forehead or had to be fetched from the police station where he had spent the night as a result of some affray. Young Martial gloried in the prestige which such incidents lent him in the eyes of his comrades.

This period did not last long, for which he felt thankful today. It came to a sudden end on the death of his father, who left him more or less alone in the world, without means of support and only half educated. At this time, however, he was within a hair's breadth of involving himself more deeply in seditious organisations and becoming a sort of professional rabble-rouser. Offers of this sort having been made to him, his natural idleness, physical toughness and pugnacious temperament almost led him to accept. It was the interest old Tournette took in him that finally deterred him.

Old Tournette! Since he was over eighty he no doubt deserved the epithet today, but Martial had always called him this, not out of mockery but on the contrary with a touch of respect. Tournette had always compelled his respect. He was a friend of his father's though he did not share his political opinions. In fact the idea that old Tournette might have political opinions of any sort seemed utterly absurd to Martial, even more absurd than if he himself had been suspected of such folly. Tournette was a photographer and nothing else. It was in this capacity that he used to accompany Martial's father on journalistic assignments. This collaboration almost always gave rise to arguments and occasionally to violent quarrels. Old Gaur, who was always inclined to give events a slant in accordance with his own opinions and those of his paper, tried to persuade Tournette that the photographs accompanying each news item should be taken in the same tendentious spirit, but the latter always stubbornly refused to comply. "The photographer must be an impartial witness," he argued. Adages of this sort, uttered in a sententious tone, had always been one of his fads.

The two men liked each other in spite of their divergent views and, when the journalist died, Tournette was the only person in the world to think of his son,

19

which was in itself extraordinary, for he was not at all inclined to bother about human beings. For a long time he had observed this wayward youth and thought that he was turning out badly. When Martial was still a child, old Tournette sometimes used to show him his collection of cameras, which included more or less every model then in existence, and explain how they worked, noticing that the boy, who seemed to take no interest in anything that really mattered, listened to what he said with unusual attention. He had even allowed him to take a few photographs, which revealed a certain instinctive ability. Subsequently, after embarking on his unruly adolescence, Martial had forgotten these lessons.

Tournette came to see him a few days after his father's death. He found him lying on his bed, chain-smoking and thinking over the offer he had just been made to become a professional agitator. The photographer made him another suggestion.

"You must decide on some profession or other. There aren't many things you can do, but you're not clumsy and you have a certain eye. Now listen. At the moment the picture departments of every paper and magazine in the country are in the process of developing at a dizzy rate. They're all short of staff, I know. They're on the lookout especially for bright, resourceful lads as press photographers. I think you could do worse for yourself than that."

"I have no training."

"I'll undertake to teach you the essentials, if you show willingness. It's a tough job, but I think you have a gift for it."

The young man thought it over for some time. The prospect of toiling every day at a regular job did not appeal to him. Tournette did not press the matter unduly.

"If you feel like it, you can always give it a try. I've brought you a camera, it's seen better days but it's still in perfect working condition. Take it with you whenever you go out. I believe you spend most of your time in the street. The street occasionally affords interesting subjects."

"What sort of subjects?"

"It's up to you to judge. That's just the point, to see if you have flair and the proper reflexes. Those are the prime qualities of a press photographer. You must be able to recognise the picture that will cause a sensation, that will merit the front page, and be quick off the mark in taking it. Sometimes it's a matter of seconds or even a fraction of a second . . . You must also know instinctively which is the best place and seize immediately on the colourful or unusual detail which will give the document a special value . . . No, don't think it's easy, but have a try."

Martial took the camera without much enthusiasm, muttering a few polite words of thanks. Yet the next day, as he was going to a meeting which was likely to prove rather stormy, he unconsciously slipped it into the pocket of the old mackintosh which he always wore for this sort of demonstration.

The meeting was even more riotous than he had expected. As it came to an end, scuffles broke out between members of the league and a group of counter-demonstrators. Being as usual in the forefront of the shock troops, Martial Gaur presently found himself in the midst of a free-for-all. Having just thrown off one opponent, he paused for breath and looked round to see where else he could make himself useful. His party seemed to be winning. A short distance away, half a dozen of his companions had cut off two of the enemy and were raining blows on them. One of them had fallen down and was trying to protect his head with his arms.

Martial fought his way towards them to be in at the death, slipping his hand into his mackintosh pocket where he usually carried his cosh. Instead, he came across Tournette's camera and pulled it out without really thinking what he was doing. He gazed at it for a moment in surprise, then stepped back a few paces and held it up to his eye, trying to focus the scene, which he managed to do after a few tentative efforts. He then followed its progress with increasing interest.

Some instinct or other prompted him to restrain his finger which was already poised on the shutter release. One of his friends was bending over the man on the ground and brandishing a club. He did not press the button until the very moment the weapon landed on the victim's face. This gave him a certain satisfaction, a sense of achievement. Then he wound on the film, still without thinking, and took another exposure showing the bloodstains on the pavement.

His gesture had passed unnoticed in the general hullabaloo. He stood there for a moment or two, as though in a day-dream, indifferent to the swirl of rioters moving further away. A fresh commotion made him raise his head. The fortunes of war seemed to have turned. He was now surrounded by enemies and the latter were hammering away at three of his comrades who were heavily outnumbered. One of them in particular was in a tight spot: a fellow by the name of Verveuil, whose fanaticism and savagery made him conspicuous at every meeting. Martial was not particularly fond of him, but he had often done battle by his side and an elementary sense of solidarity commanded him to go to his rescue. This was the rule among members of the league and he had always been quick to do so. Verveuil had caught sight of him and his eyes, blinking under a rain of blows, cried out for help.

Martial Gaur failed to react to this mute appeal. On the contrary, he stepped back three paces and trained his camera on the scene. He then paused for a moment before suddenly rushing forward. But it was not to help his companion, it was only to cross the street and take cover under a porch. He had just noticed that his earlier position presented a serious disadvantage: he was looking straight into the sun.

He took several exposures, without even hearing the curses the wretched Verveuil yelled at him. Then, as the battle again receded, he shifted his position so as to be closer to the scene of action, not as he used to do, with a show of defiance, but furtively, taking care not to get himself involved and to maintain his freedom of movement, looking all round him with a fresh eye, an eye that was indifferent to the issues at stake in this brawl, unconcerned about distinguishing friend from foe, fired only by the desire to discover some colourful element—an impartial eye, as old Tournette would say.

3

TOURNETTE CAREFULLY EXAMINED these first exposures
he had brought him. Undue praise from him was not to
be expected. He even started by criticising the range,
the angle of the shot and various other details, but
finally remarked:

"They could be worse. You have an eye and quick
reactions, just as I thought. That's already something."

Martial Gaur smiled as he recalled the pride he had
felt at this appreciation and also the joy when one of
his photographs had been published in an evening
paper.

"Now you'll have to start learning your job," Tournette had added.

He had done so. He had learnt his job with a diligence and zeal of which no one would have thought
him capable, the job of tracking down unusual material
for his camera, a quest which had taken him all over
the world, which exuded an intoxicating scent of adventure and had afforded the greatest pleasures of his
life.

He decided to go part of the way up the Boulevard

Saint-Michel on foot. He rarely undertook such long walks, which were an ordeal on account of his leg, but today the commotion in the street attracted him. He felt tempted to plunge into the crowd, as he used to do in the old days, camera in hand, every sense on the alert, in pursuit of the exceptional picture which is occasionally provided by public disturbances. This pursuit had been the main purpose of his life for almost a quarter of a century. No doubt he had never come across the unique pearl, the really sensational picture, the picture that draws tears of envy from every colleague and causes magazine owners to tremble with emotion, inducing them even to ruin themselves in order to be the first to publish it. Two or three times, however, he had come very close, and the hope of attaining it one day had kept him in a state of permanent excitement for years.

This excitement had long since abated. The scent of adventure had been replaced by the insipid perfume of the bedchamber. He was nothing more than an indoor photographer, a specialist more or less in youthful beauties in a state of undress. Alas! . . . Never would he capture the rare bird. All the same, he had to his credit two or three documents of which many of his colleagues would have been justifiably proud.

The street scene was decidedly tempting today. In the Place de la Sorbonne he noticed a tall lanky fellow perched on the roof of a car, haranguing the crowd seething round him. The orator's expression and uncontrolled gestures looked curious. He imprudently drew closer and raised his camera to his eye. A shove from behind made him lose his balance. He only just managed not to drop the instrument and had to clutch the shoulder of the man standing next to him to prevent himself from falling. That damned leg of his! He was forced to keep his eyes on the ground and watch every step he took in order to move to a quieter spot. When he was eventually able to look up again, a column of police had appeared on the scene and most of the agitators had fled. Too late! He shrugged his shoulders. When would he resign himself to the fact that this sort of photography was no longer for him? He was doomed to indoor work until the end of his days. He put the useless camera back in its case and was about to go in search of a taxi when someone gave him a tap on the shoulder.

"The young of this generation are completely gutless," said a grating voice. "In our days a couple of dozen cops wouldn't have made us take to our heels."

It was Verveuil. Martial Gaur was not surprised to run into him here, for he knew his former companion lived somewhere in the neighbourhood, had not ceased to play an active part in factious circles and was drawn to this sort of demonstration like a moth to a candle.

They had met again some time before, after losing sight of each other for several years as a result of a long estrangement. Martial shook hands with him rather diffidently. He had grudgingly agreed to a reconciliation in which he on his side could see no point.

"Why don't you take a picture of that? It would illustrate the manners of this day and age."

He indicated three or four luckless students who were being bundled into a police van.

26

"Totally uninteresting," Gaur replied impatiently. "No point in wasting a film."

"And then of course it might get you into trouble with the authorities," Verveuil went on in the same sarcastic tone. "Whatsisname wouldn't be too pleased to see a document published illustrating the behaviour of his henchmen. He's now taking children to task, the bastard!"

"Who do you mean?" said Martial absently, in a tone of complete indifference.

"Are you trying to be funny?"

But for this remark, the photographer might not have realised that the demonstration was directed against the Head of State. Verveuil, an extreme right-wing militant, felt in duty bound to be a fierce opponent of Pierre Malarche. With the malignant nature that Martial knew he had, he was probably one of those people whom the mere thought of the presidential wedding kept awake at nights. His next remark confirmed this suspicion.

"The dirty sod! Marrying a slut of twenty who's no better than she should be. That enhances the prestige of our country in the eyes of the world, doesn't it? And you think those lads aren't right to protest?"

Martial Gaur, who did not care twopence about the President and his fiancée, uttered a vague grunt by way of reply, which provoked a fresh spate of bitter recriminations from his companion.

Gaur was becoming more and more irritated. "You must admit," he said, "that the cops can't very well encourage cries of 'Malarche to the gallows!' when they're intended for the President of the Republic."

27

"That's the only treatment he deserves."

"Well, all right, if you insist. But you know . . ."

These remarks, uttered in a disillusioned tone, were fairly characteristic of Martial Gaur. Arguments of this sort seemed futile to him, and Verveuil's fanaticism struck him as sheer stupidity. This embittered, circumscribed creature was now frankly repellent to him and he cursed each chance occasion which brought them together. When they had met two or three months earlier, he on his side would willingly have prolonged the estrangement of their adolescent days. Verveuil had in fact vented his hatred on him for a long time after he had left the league, assuming the leadership of a group which accused him of cowardice and treachery. He could hardly have forgiven Martial for taking a photograph of him when he was at the mercy of his opponents, instead of coming to his rescue. For several months he had done his utmost to do him harm. Then, after some violent quarrels and even an exchange of blows, Gaur's sturdy shoulders and physical strength had eventually made him and a few other zealots of his ilk pipe down.

Yet it was Verveuil who had offered to shake hands and who had taken the first steps towards a reconciliation, to the great surprise of Martial, who knew what sort of man he was. He gave a sidelong glance at his former comrade, who continued to swear at the policemen under his breath. With his wild, deep-set eyes and pallid, angular face perpetually twisted into a sneer, Verveuil seemed to him the very model of the narrow fanatic, a species for whom he felt nothing but contempt and repulsion. Why the devil had this idiot in-

28

sisted on renewing bonds which had never been real bonds of friendship? Why had he made advances to him, evoking a past which Martial hated? Gaur was willing to bet he was not prompted by any sincere feelings. As a general rule he was fairly sceptical about feelings of this sort, and in Verveuil's case even more so. The latter, however, had commiserated on his disability, though Martial could have done without his pity. He had even offered him his services should he ever need them. After an initial terse refusal, he had insisted on being given Martial's address, declaring that old comrades-in-arms like them ought to see more of each other. It was unbelievable.

Chance, which made them near neighbours, might have facilitated their friendship. The Luxembourg alone lay between them. The photographer lived in a Montparnasse hotel, Verveuil at the top end of the Latin Quarter. Verveuil had actually called on him once or twice, then desisted, discouraged no doubt by his lack of affability.

Today, however, he was again trying to be pleasant. In spite of the obvious annoyance he felt at Martial's indifference to subjects which roused his own indignation, he eventually calmed down and went on in an indulgent tone:

"That's true. You've changed, I keep forgetting it. You're no longer keen on any cause."

"I'm a working man. I haven't the time."

After two or three rebuffs of this kind, Martial Gaur likewise calmed down and apologised for his rudeness.

"I'm sorry. I'm an invalid and I sometimes feel worn out. I'm not much good for anything these days. . . .

But what surprises me," he added with a touch of irony, indicating a fresh group marching along shouting slogans, "what surprises me is that you, who are still as fit as a fiddle and as enthusiastic as ever, aren't right up in front with those fellows."

"Why not accuse me of losing my nerve, while you're about it? Take it from me, you're wrong."

Verveuil feared more than anything in the world to be taken for a coward and this last remark had cut him to the quick. He seized Martial by the shoulder and forced him to stop.

"If I'm not marching with them, it's because there's a very good reason. Those who shout the loudest aren't always the most useful to a cause."

"That's what I've always thought myself. Don't be so touchy. All I meant was . . ."

But Verveuil would not let him get away with it so easily and insisted on exonerating himself.

"You don't believe me, do you? I swear that if you knew the importance of the activity on which I'm engaged, you'd never cast aspersions like that on me."

He noticed he had raised his voice so that several passers-by by turned round and stared. He stopped abruptly, his face clouded over, then continued walking.

"I can't tell you more about it. There are too many interests at stake and you wouldn't understand."

It was now Martial Gaur's turn to be annoyed. He could not suppress a shrug of his shoulders. It was typical of Verveuil to indulge in this mysterious manner intended to suggest he was an important figure in possession of state secrets.

"Good heavens, of course I believe you!" he exclaimed. "And I'm not asking you to tell me any more. As I said before, I'm no longer interested in all that."

They parted company a few minutes later, after Verveuil had again lavished all sorts of civilities on him, as if he had forgotten all about their argument. He even helped Gaur into a taxi and would not let him drive off until he had asked once again how he was getting on, what sort of life he was leading, whether he was not too lonely, whether he had any friends—a solicitude which Gaur could not help regarding as hypocritical.

4

Every sign of unrest disappeared as soon as he was on the other side of the Luxembourg. Old Montparnasse seemed to disdain such uncontrolled exuberance and Martial Gaur felt in perfect mental communion with his district.

Back in his hotel, he went into the bar to see if Herst, whom he was expecting that evening, had arrived. Herst had not yet turned up. No doubt the atmosphere of unrest that reigned in Paris was complicating his task. He thought of waiting for him in the bar, then changed his mind and went up to his room after leaving a message for his friend.

The hotel, situated in a little side-street not far from Notre-Dame-des-Champs, was quiet and reasonably comfortable. The photographer had been a long-standing client. He always used to stay here in the old days, between one assignment and another, and had made it his permanent residence since he had stopped travelling.

Having reached his landing, he stopped outside the room next to his. It was Olga's room. Since he had been stirring up dusty old memories for more than an hour, it might be as well if he sought some other distraction.

32

He paused for a moment outside the door, undecided whether to knock or not, the picture of Olga in his mind's eye driving away the ghosts of the past.

A strange girl, Olga. Olga . . . Poulain, he was not sure he had remembered her surname correctly. Pleasant enough, no doubt, but there was something odd about her. He recollected the way she had flung herself into his arms a few days earlier, which had caused him an astonishment from which he had not yet recovered.

He wondered for the umpteenth time what she could have seen in him, Martial Gaur, a pretty misanthropic fellow, crotchety, no longer young and a cripple into the bargain. Some of the starlets among his clients occasionally made advances to him and he had sometimes taken advantage of this, but in their case there was an obvious motive, as he realised only too well—the hope of obtaining from him a series of photographs which would be particularly flattering to them. In his specialised field, which he often cursed but on which he brought all his professional qualifications to bear, he had in fact acquired a reputation equal to that of the leading studios.

It was certainly not this sort of interest that had prompted Olga. She asked him no favours. She was neither an actress nor a cover-girl. Her job was not connected in any way with photography: she worked in an antique shop. At least that is what he thought he remembered her telling him. He did not give a straw for these particulars.

She had been staying at the hotel for about a month. They had got to know each other in the bar, where they sometimes came to write their letters, after having met by chance once or twice in the lift. He had noticed a certain gravity, not to say harshness in her demeanour, which contrasted with her youthful figure (she could not be more than twenty-five) and somewhat unprepossessing face, strangely animated at times by a fleeting gleam which appeared in her singularly deep-set eyes. It made a nice change from the little hussies he saw every day. Furthermore, there was an intriguing factor which aroused his curiosity about this girl, endowing her with an enigmatic quality: he was sure he had seen her face somewhere before and almost certain it had been in a photograph. His professional eye had an infallible memory in such matters. But where he had registered the features of this countenance (she was no doubt younger at the time; he seemed to recall a childish expression) he was utterly unable to remember, and he felt that all his efforts in this direction would be in vain.

They had had a drink together. With a smile she had then told him (this was another cause for surprise) that she knew him by name and by repute. She clearly remembered, she said, a certain photograph he had taken during the Indo-China War which she had seen in a popular magazine.

He himself of course remembered this photograph, one of the gems of his collection. His pride had been flattered and he had gone so far as to tell her more about himself. In the isolation and obscurity in which he was living, it was difficult for him to remain insensible to such a sign of interest. All the same, as he subsequently recalled this incident, he could not help considering it strange. That someone should remember an outstanding picture (which this one was), well and

34

good (and yet how old could she have been during the Indo-China War? A mere child!); but to remember the name of the photographer seemed highly improbable. A photographer never attains the notoriety of a painter, alas! Even in the case of a really sensational picture, his name remains in the memory of a mere handful of specialists, fellow professionals, and even then not for very long. Yet she had mentioned specific details and the approximate date of its publication. . . . An absolute phenomenon of a woman! And this memory of hers could not even be ascribed to a deep interest in the art of photography in general. He had quickly realised she knew nothing about the subject and was unaware of the two or three documents which were considered really worth while in the realm of press photography.

"After all, maybe my physical appearance originally appealed to her and then she informed herself about me in order to induce me to share her feelings by playing on my vanity," he told himself, still pondering on this anomaly. Despite the improbability of this explanation, it was still the only reasonable one he could find. In any case it was rather a pleasant sop to his pride.

He happened to mention by chance a certain series of what in his opinion were his best pictures, many of which had for various reasons never been published. She asked him to show them to her. He kept them in a drawer, never allowed anyone to see them and hardly ever looked at them himself. She manifested such a friendly persistence that he could not get out of it. He took her up to his room, which by chance was next to hers, and, after getting out his album, found himself again evoking further memories, with something of his former enthusiasm which had been revived by the sympathy she showed.

He spoke for a long time, almost without looking at her, each picture giving birth to a fresh story. As he came to the last exposure (of the rebel responsibility for his disability) Olga's gaze met his and he fancied he saw in her eyes an emotion akin to his own. It had seemed so to him at the moment, maybe because he had grown unaccustomed to situations of this kind. Thinking it over afterwards, and again today—he had a mania for retracing in his mind certain manifestations that had disturbed him and analysing them in order to discover a reason for them—this emotion seemed to him difficult to explain. He would start suspecting her of shamming and feigning, with an almost diabolical ability, sentiments which she did not feel. The next moment he would reproach himself for such an assumption.

Whatever her feelings or reasons may have been, she had fallen quite naturally into his arms and become his mistress. It had been as simple as that. He particularly liked simplicity, and she too seemed to appreciate it. All the same, it was odd, he said to himself, as he pondered on their relationship. But no doubt it was his own character that impelled him to regard a perfectly normal attitude as strange. It was becoming an obsession with him. Earlier on, he had been inclined to consider Verveuil's civilities almost suspect and hypocritical. And here he was now reading ulterior motives into the impulsive gesture of an infatuated woman. No one but himself, Martial Gaur, would remain permanently on his guard like this.

36

He gave a characteristic shrug and after another pause silently entered his own room, abandoning the idea of knocking on Olga's door. After all, he had plenty of time to see her, this evening, or maybe tomorrow if Herst was late in leaving. He had to give her credit on this point: she did not complicate his existence in any way, the existence of a rather crusty old bachelor jealous of his independence, and for this he felt profoundly grateful to her. He enjoyed being alone when he felt like it and could not have tolerated a woman meddling in his life at every moment. There was nothing to fear on this score from Olga Poulain, if that was indeed her name. She had no wish to importune or fetter him and had made a point of telling him so, which had been a fresh cause for astonishment to him.

She seemed content to spend a few hours with him from time to time, without ever imposing her presence on him. Not once so far had she asked him to take her out for the evening, nor had she ever expressed the slightest wish to meet his friends, who were in any case limited in number: three or four bohemians like himself, such as Herst, who at the age of forty or fifty continued to lead the life of superannuated students and whose favourite pastimes were bridge, billiards and chess in the smoky atmosphere of the Left Bank cafés.

"The ideal woman for me, on the whole," he muttered as he laid his equipment on his bed.

It was an obvious statement of fact, but the many qualities he recognised in her still impelled him to regard the coincidence that had brought them together as strange.

37

5

THE RINGING OF THE TELEPHONE surprised him while he was still thinking of Olga as he shuffled about in a dressing-gown after having a shower. It was Herst, who had just arrived.

"Is that you? I'm just changing. I've had a hard day. I'll be ready in ten minutes. Will you wait in the bar or come up here?"

Herst told him not to hurry. He had just looked in to pass the time of day, since he was not free to dine with him this evening as they had planned.

"Then come up, and tell the barman to bring us something to drink. You can spare five minutes, can't you?"

When he opened the door he fancied he heard a faint noise in the adjoining room. Olga was surely there and could hear him letting his friend in. But she would keep to herself, as usual, without revealing her presence. He smiled: this was what he liked about her. He would have behaved in the same way himself in similar circumstances. After all, this mutual understanding ought to be able to take the place of love, which nowadays he was utterly incapable of feeling and which he still suspected her of keeping separate from her usual cares in spite of her marks of affection.

"How's our friend Malarche? Not assassinated yet?"

This was the traditional joke with which he greeted his friend. A former parachute sergeant-major, who had subsequently tried out a number of adventurous jobs in civilian life, including professional boxing and all-in wrestling, Herst today had an unusual profession. To his friends he described himself as "Chief Thug of the Republic". In fact he was head of the bodyguard which accompanied the President on his tours and official ceremonies. At certain times this was no sinecure.

"The President's as fit as a fiddle."

"I was pretty sure you wouldn't be free this evening. You must have your hands full, with all these disturbances."

"It's not the rowdy demonstrations that worry me. On the contrary, at the moment he's lying low and not appearing in public, so I'm not responsible for his security. When there's an apparent lull and he puts his nose outside, however—that's when I start trembling in my shoes. You won't be seeing much of me next week. And this evening I have to attend a meeting of the big shots who have to draw up a general plan and allocate our various tasks for the ceremony."

"The ceremony? Next week?"

"Don't tell me you don't know the President's getting married next week?"

"I'd forgotten."

Herst raised his eyes to the ceiling and uttered a few

39

sarcastic remarks about artists living immured in their
ivory towers without ever devoting a single thought to
events that concern the rest of mankind. Then he flung
his mackintosh down on the bed and lowered his muscu-
lar frame into the only armchair in the room.

"You know, as far as I'm concerned, the President's
wedding . . ."

"I know, I know. You don't give a damn about it."

Without a pause, as frequently happened when he
was with his friend, Herst gave free rein to the torrent
of worries that beset this final stage of his career.

"If only he'd agree to a simple ceremony, in private,
it would irritate his opponents less in the first place.
There'd be less chitter-chatter and, apart from that, it
would be easier for us to keep an eye on him. But no,
not him! You don't know what he's like. It's when the
atmosphere is most electric that he insists on flaunting
himself and confronting his opponents in public. He
insists on a big ceremony, with all the frills. A church
wedding, which makes the bigots cry sacrilege; a procession, with himself in the forefront of course. And if
we get too close when he's surrounded by the crowd,
he'll tell us to clear off as usual."

"But do you really think his life's in danger?"

"If I had anything definite to go on, it wouldn't be
so bad. I only know what is common knowledge, that
thousands of Frenchmen hate his guts and would give
a great deal to put paid to him. In this sort of atmosphere there are some presidents who live to a ripe old
age and die in bed. There are others who are put out of
the way at the very start of their career. This is the
situation. The Security Department have notified us of

40

disturbing rumours and advised us to keep a closer watch than ever. Only he himself prevents us from applying strict measures. He insists on direct contact with the masses—his trump card according to him. Maybe it's true, but sometimes it's sheer madness. And so . . ."

"And so?" echoed Martial, who was only half listening.

"Keep this under your hat, of course. Outside the church there'll be the customary photographs, any amount of photographs in fact. Press photographers from all over the world will be there. You can't see your colleagues missing an occasion like this, can you? He himself is delighted; he likes to pose. And that little nitwit of a fiancée of his enjoys it even more. His pleasure and glory won't be complete if his wedding takes place without popular acclaim and photographs. The session is bound to last a long time, several minutes probably. Well, he insists on our keeping out of the way while it's going on. Yes, he doesn't find us sufficiently photogenic, I suppose. We mustn't appear in these pictures. Sheer vanity, as usual. Can't you imagine it? The church square seething with people and himself swaggering on the steps above the crowd . . . the sort of target a child of ten couldn't miss!"

Martial had taken a little more interest in the conversation at the mention of photography.

"All the same," he said ironically, "I suppose the balconies on the square will be kept under surveillance and there'll be several plain-clothes men among the crowd?"

"Of course, but it's impossible to think of everything," said Herst, almost in desperation. "Naturally the buildings opposite the church will be under surveillance, but we can't go nosing into every house in the district. Besides, if you only knew how the whole thing's organised! There are at least three other branches which deal with security, apart from my own, not to mention certain highly placed persons who don't understand a thing about it but who must at all costs have their say and give their opinion. In consequence we find ourselves relying on the others without knowing exactly what steps they have taken. That's what they call distribution of responsibility, in other words complete and utter chaos. I can't sleep any longer. I lie awake at night imagining myself in the position of a potential killer, to try and guess from which direction the danger may come."

He broke off for a moment while the barman brought in a bottle and some glasses, then went on listing his problems in a distraught voice. Good old Herst! Martial Gaur felt great affection for him and understood his anxiety even though he was incapable of sharing it. The henchman was coming to the end of his career. He was over forty-five and had only been kept on because of Pierre Malarche himself, who had known him in the old days and was fond of him; but it was obvious he could not stay on much longer. On the eve of his retirement, a successful attempt against the President would have been regarded by him as a personal dishonour.

Herst drained his glass in rapid gulps, bleakly watching Martial as he dressed. He refused another drink and got up. He wanted to have a clear head for his interview with the authorities and went off after they had arranged to dine together on the following evening.

"I'll let you know what pearls of wisdom are dropped in the course of the meeting. Enough for a dilettante like you to laugh his head off, no doubt."

Martial accompanied him as far as the lift, then came back slowly and paused again outside Olga's door. He was now free for the evening and felt like asking her out. But he could not make up his mind; it was one of those days when he needed to be alone.

He returned to his own room without making a sound and sat down in the armchair with his eyes fixed on the album he had shown Olga several days before, which was still lying on the table. It contained a pictorial record of the most exciting period of his career: wartime. He picked it up unconsciously and sighed as he turned over a leaf. It began in 1939 and ended with the Algerian War.

6

IN 1939, THE DECLARATION OF WAR threw Martial Gaur into a state of feverish excitement which had nothing to do with patriotism. It was simply the manifestation of a particular aesthetic sense: events were no doubt going to enable him to take pictures worthy of him, worthy of the art of photography which he had been practising for three years and in which he felt he was a pastmaster.

The first year brought him little but disappointment. He had succeeded in enlisting as a war photographer but found nothing of interest to bite on. The pictures he was commissioned to take nauseated him: generals in battledress inspecting advanced posts and doling out cigarettes to the soldiers, organisation of the warriors' off-duty hours, army theatricals... The sickening banality of these pictures drove him to despair and he viewed the phoney war with an indignation akin to the sentiments animating the most bellicose supporters of the offensive.

Came the catastrophe, the German advance of 1940, which put new heart into him! The French defeat even

infected him with the feverish tremor, the heady mixture of hope and nervous anxiety, which to the artist
heralds a great achievement. Unquestioningly, he ap-
plied old Tournette's favourite precepts: the photographer must be impartial; the photographer must be
just; a just man has no preconceived opinion. A disas-
ter on the enemy side would have provoked more or
less the same reactions in him, albeit slightly tempered
by the greater difficulty of recording certain aspects of
it on film.

The French defeat thus afforded him unhoped-for
opportunities, which he did not allow to slip through his
fingers.... This series of photographs, for instance.
They were one of his earlier triumphs. As he looked at
them this evening he was almost moved to tears, recol-
lecting the pride and joy they had given him. They had
been taken in the darkest hours of defeat. The unit to
which he was attached was first of all pulverised by a
squadron of Stukas and, from the hole in which he
had taken cover, he was able to take some striking
exposures of the damage, in particular the explosion of
an ammunition dump which caused hundreds of casu-
alties.

Then the enemy armoured columns appeared on
the scene. Here he had a real stroke of luck, as he himself admitted. He was able to get a close-up of the track
of one of the biggest tanks as it reared up in the air
and fell back onto a mass of wounded men cowering
at the bottom of a trench. The angle of the exposure
was almost perfect. The desperate expression on the
poor fellows' faces was something quite exceptional.

Finally the German infantry arrived and fortune

45

continued to smile on him. This really was his hour of glory. He felt he had thoroughly deserved it, after kicking his heels for so long. He had managed to get a snap of the colonel in command of his unit just as the latter was raising his arms in surrender, horrified by the human tide sweeping towards him.

His star continued to shine throughout that auspicious day, for he managed to escape and bring back all these documents to base, where they caused quite a sensation. Many of them, alas, could not be published at the time. His disappointment was tempered, however, by the envy they aroused among the professionals who heard about them.

The next few pages of the album were devoted to the occupation. He consented to join a Resistance group, but only on condition that he was allowed to pursue his career. This condition was accepted; the Resistance needed photographers. First of all, and at the risk of his life, he took various pictures of enemy installations which were of particular value to the allied air forces. But he was only half interested in this sort of activity. Fortunately there were livelier incidents, as illustrated by one print showing a group of German police kicking a woman marked with the yellow star. This had been widely used for propaganda purposes and had the honour of being sent to London and published in several newspapers. It earned him congratulations and a decoration, since he had taken the greatest risks to obtain it.

Then there was another print, showing an act of violence perpetrated this time by the Resistance. To operate, he had had to steer clear of his own friends at the time. This print too had of course been kept on the secret files. He had only shown it, later on, to a few reliable cronies, objective specialists, "just" men like Tournette, who were able to appreciate art for art's sake in matters of photography.

Herst appeared in one of these photographs. It was at this time he had first met him and become attached to him. Herst was then quite young (seventeen at the most) but his stamina, pugnacity and physical constitution made him a valuable man in action. They had become friends, despite profound differences of character. The one point they had in common was the eagerness with which they sought out the most dangerous spots, Martial Gaur from professional necessity and an ever more fervent desire for spectacular pictures, Herst from patriotism, natural courage and love of adventure. The photographer, because of his greater maturity and intellectual superiority, soon exercised an ascendancy over his companion who until then had seen little of the world apart from physical training centres and sports clubs. Frequently, having been informed in advance of some hazardous operation in which he was due to take part, Herst, who had finally understood and accepted what his friend was after, would show him the best spot in which to position himself, believing that the role of the photographer was even more important than his own for the cause they were serving.

This quest for perilous situations brought them together again afterwards, the subsequent wars attracting them both for the same reasons as before. Martial Gaur had not missed a single one—first of all Korea, then Indo-China and finally Algeria, which had put an end to his career. Herst, after a brief incursion into civilian life, had been through Indo-China and Algeria in a parachute unit. Gaur, whose particular job was bound to take him to the most interesting sectors, thus re-encountered his old Resistance friend in the middle of a battle, when he had just been promoted to sergeant-major for gallantry in the field. Once again Herst was able to give him inside information which enabled him to make straight for a key position from which he could take a first-rate photograph. . . . Good old Herst! Martial was really extremely fond of him. He and Tournette had remained his closest friends. But Tournette was now very old and almost blind, though he still continued to practise his art, without ever moving from his room, endeavouring to create within four walls, by a subtle combination of materials, the outstanding composition which he could no longer contrive out of doors, somewhat as Martial Gaur himself was now reduced to doing.

He had come to the last picture, the one he had mentioned that afternoon to the starlet, the one he had taken while pouring with blood and with his leg shattered by bullets. He could not bring himself to look at it and abruptly closed the album.

Thus it was that Martial Gaur had moved from one trouble spot to another, playing in every conflict a singular role, the role of an impartial observer, with the same equally divided contempt for beliefs, opinions and parties, the same ethical indifference to ignoble acts and meritorious acts, feats of valour and feats of cowardice, only working himself up into a state of enthusiasm, but then to the highest degree, when human passions revealed themselves through outstanding images which were sufficiently evocative and unusual to justify a photograph.

He tossed the album on to the bed next to his camera and sat for a long time without moving, gazing at a spot on the wall between the adjoining room and his own. He was roused from his reverie by Olga's voice, which he could faintly hear on the other side. He pricked up his ears but could not catch a single word. She was speaking on the telephone and he could only discern a vague murmur.

He was sitting there, still in a state of indecision, unable to make up his mind whether to go and see her or not, when a strange impression made him furtively crane his neck, blink his eyes, then wrinkle his brow, as though he had just noticed some incongruous sight.

7

THE OBJECT WHICH HAD ATTRACTED his attention, and on which his gaze had accidentally been fixed for the last moment or two, was so trivial that at first he reproached himself for allowing himself to be distracted by a detail that was probably of no significance at all.

It was a coil of electric wires emerging from a rubber tube which went through the wall, then ran along the edge of the skirting-board and disappeared behind the cupboard. Only an eye like his, a photographer's eye, professionally trained to grasp every detail of a scene in an instant, could have discerned the unusual aspect. Yet he was certain he was not mistaken. He had contemplated this coil too often with disapproval, deploring the habit of the old artisans who left these far from decorative accessories uncovered instead of concealing them in the masonry. Originally there had been only three wires there; his eye had registered the diameter of the coil. Today it looked slightly larger.

He got up and struggled into a sitting position on the floor. His eye had not deceived him; the coil now consisted of four wires instead of three. He had no difficulty in recognising the latest addition: it was about the same colour as the others, but it did not have the same patina. He crawled round to the other side of the cupboard and spotted where the wires reappeared. At this point there were only three of them: the three original ones.

His frown grew more pronounced. He went back to his first position, lay down flat on the floor and ran his hand along the coil. It was not long before he discovered the cause of the mystery. The additional wire did not go very far. His fingers were arrested by a small object which appeared to be fixed to the wall behind the cupboard. This seemed sufficiently strange for him to go to the trouble of removing it, taking care not to make a sound. The object he unearthed was familiar to him, he had seen others like it in the course of his adventurous life; it was a tiny microphone scarcely larger than a thimble.

His past experience of hazardous and unexpected incidents saved Martial Gaur on this occasion from acting hurriedly. He kept his head completely and, apart from a faint whistle of surprise, made no sound at this discovery. He took care not to touch the apparatus. As soon as he recognised it for what it was, he replaced it behind the cupboard as silently as he had removed it, sat down again in the armchair and started thinking, more or less in the same position as before but indulging in very different reflections.

The wire came from Olga's room, which she had occupied for about a month, and Gaur was certain it had not been there a few days earlier. No reconstruction had been undertaken on this floor of the hotel for some time. There was no other conclusion to be drawn: Olga herself had installed the microphone, taking advantage of a couple of occasions on which she had been alone in his room since the start of their affair. She was spying on him. This was the reason, without any doubt, why she had been so eager to fling herself at him. This was the explanation for her apparent infatuation.

While his natural scepticism rejoiced at discovering an ulterior motive for an apparently spontaneous act, he felt slightly resentful, for it was a blow to his self-esteem. He had been ready to humour her; he would not be taken in again. She had surrendered to him in order to spy on him at her leisure. This was all it amounted to.

But his feelings of disillusion were quickly dispelled by excitement at the fresh enigma which now obtruded on his mind and shrouded the girl's conduct in a mist still thicker than before his discovery. Why the devil should she wish to spy on him, Martial Gaur, a solitary old recluse who led a life that was as clear as daylight and who was uninterested in all topical affairs? This seemed even more unaccountable than her infatuation.

Was she mistaking him for someone else? The now obvious fact that she had informed herself about him before approaching him precluded this hypothesis. Did she believe him to be in possession of some important secret? He vowed to solve this problem as soon as possible. Now that his mind was made up, he decided to go and see her then and there, without of course mentioning his discovery.

*

Olga took only a few seconds to open her door but he noticed it had been locked and bolted. She was obviously about to go out, for she was wearing an overcoat and her bag was on the bed beside her gloves.

Their embrace was a perfect sample of duplicity. He derived a strange sort of pleasure from assessing according to certain symptoms to what degree his mistress's nerves and muscles were exercised in feigning affection. As for himself, while pressing his body against hers and covering her face with kisses, with every sign of the most ingenuous passion, he forced her to step back slightly so as to draw closer to the wall. Then, while he planted a kiss on the back of her neck, he looked over her shoulder searching for the spot where the electric wires emerged.

It was not long before he spotted it, not far from a cupboard similar to the one in his own room. There were likewise four wires there, he could have sworn, and the coil disappeared in the same way behind the piece of furniture. He felt fresh satisfaction at discerning some marks on the carpet. This was enough for him: the suspect wire obviously stopped behind the cupboard. He could easily imagine her, as she was about to eavesdrop on him, taking the loose end of the wire and connecting it to some earphones or a recording device. He would have given a great deal to have a look through one of her suitcases. It seemed to have a solid lock, but the key lay near-by on a low table. The marks on the carpet no doubt came from this table, which had been shifted.

These marks were fresh. It occurred to him, as he kissed her on the lips, that she had probably listened in to his conversation with Herst, but for the moment he attached no particular importance to this.

"Have you been in long? Why didn't you knock on my door?" he asked her in a friendly tone of reproach.

This was a somewhat odd remark for him to make, considering their tacit agreement never to impose themselves on each other; but he had decided to be particularly amiable.

"I thought I heard voices in your room. I assumed you had a visitor and didn't want to bother you."

He had drawn away from her and was now looking her straight in the eye, his hands on her shoulders, closely studying her reactions while continuing to smile with the greatest affection. She met his gaze and her face reflected an equally tender smile. He could not help admiring her presence of mind: if she had pretended not to have heard anything in the next room, it might have aroused his suspicions.

"It was only Herst, one of my closest friends. I must introduce him to you some day. . . . He has a rather unusual job, he's a personal bodyguard, attached to the Head of State."

A vague intuition had prompted him to talk of Herst and his profession, while he continued to study her reactions. She did not frown but he fancied he noticed a faint tremor in her shoulder. He went no further and changed the subject.

"Were you going out? I thought that maybe this evening . . ."

For a moment or two he had had the impression that his visit was upsetting Olga's plans, that she was in a hurry to leave and, without being able to explain why or how, that this departure of hers was connected with the telephone conversation he had indistinctly overheard shortly before.

"I thought maybe we might have dinner together this evening... unless you're otherwise engaged, of course."

He made this suggestion with the vague idea of embarrassing her, so firm was his conviction that she had an urgent appointment. A shadow of vexation passed over Olga's face and she looked away.

"If only I'd known . . . But listen . . ."

She had recovered herself at once. He had not been mistaken in crediting her with an outstanding control over her emotions.

"I was going out to see a colleague from my shop who just rang me up."

This was a blatant lie. It gave him intense satisfaction to realise that she was not infallible, in spite of her ability, even because of her sharpness, which had prompted her to mention this telephone call which he might have overheard. But she had spoken too quickly. It had not been an incoming call. The ringing was perfectly audible between one room and the other and he was sure he had not heard it. It was a blunder on her part, which he was too observant to miss. He had scored a hit in this fencing match on which they had embarked this evening. It was she who had rung up, believing no doubt that Martial had gone out with Herst. This lie confirmed his suspicion that there was something fishy about this conversation.

"I quite understand," he said rather hypocritically. "If you've promised . . ."

"But I don't really want to see this friend. Give me a moment and I'll put her off. Yes, yes, I assure you, I particularly want to go out with you this evening."

"In that case . . ."

She kissed him again and went over to the telephone, where she hesitated slightly since he remained standing by the door. He was tempted to stay there, just to embarrass her, but this attitude was liable to arouse her suspicions, which was something he particularly wanted to avoid. Furthermore, it would serve no purpose. He felt she was sufficiently adroit to find some means of averting this conversation in his presence.

"I'll wait for you in the bar."

He went off down the corridor. A shadow appeared on the wall opposite her door, which was still open: she was making quite sure he was taking the lift. He made no attempt to spy on her but, on reaching the ground floor, went straight to the cubby-hole used by the telephone operator, an old friend of his whom he had known for over twenty years, ever since he had first stayed in this hotel. In those days she had been a chamber-maid. Subsequently, crippled by rheumatism, she had been enabled to continue to earn her living thanks to this job at the switchboard.

Gaur had done her several favours, lending her money when she was hard up and taking flattering photographs, for which he charged her nothing, of one of her nieces who wanted to make a career in films. He could be capable of charitable gestures when they did not reflect on his profession. There was nothing she would not do for him.

"Hand me the earphones. Yes, Number Twenty-Two. I want to hear what she's saying."

"What does it matter to you? Are you jealous? That's not like you at all."

His affair with Olga was known to every member of the staff. At first she made as though to object, then she shrugged her shoulders, pointed to the earphones and looked away.

"Go ahead. I'm not watching you."

Even before grasping the sense of the words, Gaur gave a gasp of astonishment. The voice of the man speaking to Olga was familiar to him. He was sure he had heard it quite recently. This was his first impression, but he still hesitated to assign a name to the mystery man, so fantastic did it appear to him. It was an overbearing voice with an unpleasant grating tone.

"So you can't meet me this evening? All right. I leave you free to act for the best."

Martial gasped again and the old telephone operator glanced at him anxiously. The name of the man on the other end of the line asserted itself with every word. Olga was now speaking.

"I thought it better not to refuse his invitation. We must win his confidence. Besides, I may gather some additional details which escaped me this evening. I couldn't hear everything."

The man's voice broke in abruptly:

"No point in going into that again now. You gave me the main facts earlier on. I have no objection, I tell you. It's up to you to take the proper steps."

It was Verveuil! There was no longer any possible

57

doubt. Martial recognised not only the voice but the bombastic tone.

"Till tomorrow, then," Verveuil went on. "Meanwhile I'm going to make a few arrangements. One o'clock tomorrow, on a bench in the Luxembourg, on the Rue Guynemer side, beyond the croquet lawn."

"Right."

The conversation was over. Martial Gaur laid down the earphones and hurried off to the bar after giving the operator a friendly tap on the shoulder by way of thanks. He sat down on a stool, as though in a daze, without even hearing the barman's greeting.

What the devil did this mean? In what fantastic adventure was he once again involved? It looked very much like a conspiracy. For what shady undertaking was Olga associated with Verveuil? It was Verveuil, without any doubt, who had set the girl on his heels; he recalled many details which confirmed this view: the apparently fortuitous encounter with that silly fool some two months previously, his insistence on being given his address, on knowing what sort of life he led and on renewing their relations. It was a little later that Olga had moved to the hotel, probably because Verveuil had realised that he himself would never be admitted into the circle of his intimate associates, with the obvious mission of worming her way into his confidence, spying on him, listening into his conversations with his friends, with . . .

With Herst especially. It was getting clearer and clearer. The conversation to which she had referred on the telephone was certainly the one he had had with the bodyguard. It was in order to report it to her accomplice, to her boss more likely, that she had rung up immediately afterwards, fixing a rendezvous with him that very evening. What had they said that was so important? Herst had kept harping on his professional worries, on the anxiety he was caused by the public appearances of the Head of State, and especially next week's wedding ceremony. Good heavens! . . .

He had reached this point in his reflections and deductions when Olga appeared on the threshold of the bar. He rose to greet her and watched her approaching him. Her thin, almost imperceptible lips were softened by a tender smile, her face embellished by the unusual gleam that sometimes came into her dark eyes, in which he could read only the pleasure she anticipated at spending an evening with her lover.

8

ON A BENCH IN THE LUXEMBOURG, near one of the lawns along the Rue Guynemer reserved for lovers of peace and quiet, Olga Poulain sat munching a sandwich, occasionally crumbling up some bits of bread for the sparrows hovering round her. There were few people about at this time of the day. The benches near hers were unoccupied. The few frequenters of this haven kept a reasonable distance from one another, as though abiding by some tacit agreement.

This atmosphere of tranquillity did not prevent Verveuil from darting suspicious glances in every direction and walking round the lawn twice with affected nonchalance before coming and sitting down beside her. While this was going on, she pretended not to notice him, diligently following the instructions he had given her, even though they were obviously puerile. Olga felt no consideration for Verveuil, whom she rated at his proper value, but the fanaticism of this imbecile served her purpose. They had in fact only one sentiment in common: deadly hatred towards the same person. The reason for this hatred was quite different for each of them, but it sufficed to associate them both in a close collaboration.

She forced herself not to look round at Verveuil as he sat down on the bench and to muster all her patience in order to go through the performance on which he insisted at each of their rendezvous. He began by blinking one eye three or four times, then ventured to utter some trite remark about the weather, to which she did not reply at first, doing so only at his insistence and with cold reserve, like a woman accosted by a stranger. It was only after several minutes of this charade that she appeared to relent. Then he shifted closer to her and they embarked on a conversation in undertones, during which he never ceased to inspect the immediate surroundings.

"So Herst came yesterday evening, did he? He talked about the ceremony and you were able to overhear part of their conversation?"

"I heard almost all of it."

"Let's have your report, then. The main points first of all."

She gave an account of the conversation between the two friends, outlining the main points as he demanded, namely the ceremony of the presidential wedding, the security measures to be adopted, and the henchman's anxiety on this score.

"It's as clear as daylight. Malarche wants to appear in full view of the crowd. He'll pose for the photographers outside the church, in the forefront of the procession. This will last several minutes and the bodyguards will have to keep out of the way all the time. A perfect target, as Herst himself admits. Furthermore, there's a lot of bickering among the various departments responsible for security, who don't see eye to eye about the measures to be taken. We'll never have such an opportunity as this."

Verveuil listened with a self-important air, wrinkling his brow like a man of authority.

"It seems to be shaping up nicely," he finally said. "But didn't Herst give any details about these measures?"

"Yes. Close watch will be kept on the houses in the square itself and at the end of the avenue facing it. As for the other streets branching out from there, they're concerned only about the house fronts affording a view of the church steps. This doesn't apply to the street in which we're interested. It will be completely neglected. The church can't be seen from any of the windows."

"But it can be seen quite clearly from the scaffolding," Verveuil murmured, lowering his voice still further and after making sure again that no one could hear them. "I checked that myself yesterday."

"Yes, it can be seen from the scaffolding and that's our chance. But the police aren't likely to think of that."

"That's what you say."

"That's what I say, and don't forget I've known the police all my life," she said in a harsh voice. "They're all the same: oafs and imbeciles who carry out orders without thinking. . . . Anyway," she went on, changing her tone, "the final plan must have been drawn up during last night's conference. I'll hear about it, if not over the microphone, then from Gaur himself. Herst confides in him completely and he's becoming more and more attached to me. Last night he told me everything that had been said in the course of their conversation and even gave me further details which I had missed. It's a topic that seems to amuse him and I only have to sit back and listen."

"The little bitch!" Martial Gaur muttered, clenching his teeth.

Seated on a stool in a truck parked in the Rue Guynemer alongside the gardens—a truck that was hermetically sealed except for a tiny opening—Gaur had for some time been squinting through the lens of a strange instrument carefully trained on the bench occupied by the two accomplices. The truck had been lent to him by a friend, a television technician. It was generally put into service for the "Invisible Eye" programme and it was not the first time Gaur had borrowed it. He had used it whenever he wanted to take photographs and at the same time remain unnoticed. But today it was not a camera that was concealed in the vehicle, it was an equally indiscreet but less common instrument.

It was encased in a rectangular box with sloping sides the size of an ordinary typewriter, equipped in front with a sort of funnel surmounted by a viewfinder. The funnel was simply the earpiece of an extremely sensitive microphone known to certain specialists as "ultra-directional". The box contained a powerful amplifier. The lens served to place the earpiece accurately in line with the mouth of the person one wished to overhear.

This instrument was hardly ever used outside police

and Secret Service circles, but old Tournette owned one, which he had acquired regardless of the fairly heavy expense, obsessed by his collecting mania which was becoming more pronounced the older he grew and which extended to every apparatus consisting of some optical device or other, even if unconnected with photography. He had lent it this morning to Martial, accepting the latter's casual explanation that the ultra-directional microphone would be useful to him for obtaining information with a view to a sensational picture. The old boy was unable to resist an argument of this kind, as Gaur knew only too well. He had handed over his museum piece after explaining its manipulation, which was simple, and adding a mass of technical details about its mechanism which were above Martial's head.

What interested him was that a clear reception was guaranteed up to two hundred yards, in theory. In practice it was safer not to exceed half this distance. He was at present well within this range, so that he did not miss a single word uttered by the conspirators despite the care they took not to raise their voices.

"The little bitch!" he exclaimed again. "And a silly little fool as well. She takes me for an idiot."

The evening before, during dinner, he had indeed given her an account of his conversation with Herst, without omitting a single detail; but this was certainly not ingenuousness on his part. All the time he was complacently conversing, he had kept on the alert for signs of special attention on her part and desire to find out more, a desire which she concealed to the best of her ability under an outward appearance of indifference, avoiding asking any questions. All the jokes he made about his friend's job and present anxiety were merely feelers designed to detect her own reactions.

She was a good actress, no doubt, but, once again, too perfect. Any other woman would have had her curiosity aroused by these revelations and would have kept asking for further details. Such exemplary discretion was, in his eyes, proof of a particular interest.

"It's decided," Verveuil suddenly said with a determined gesture. "It will be for next Saturday, during the photography session outside the church. In eight days from now France will be rid of that wretch."

Gaur perceived a touch of anxiety in Olga's expression and voice.

"You're sure not to miss?"

Verveuil assumed a superior air and gave a little chuckle of self-satisfaction.

"My dear girl, don't forget that for a long time I've been considered a first-class shot and you may as well know I haven't lost my eye. I practise every week. With telescopic sights I wouldn't miss an orange at a hundred yards, and it's no more than eighty between our scaffolding and the church door."

"The swine!" Martial Gaur muttered, clutching his instrument.

The tone in which he uttered this exclamation betrayed little indignation, however. He was too stupefied to feel indignant. Astonishment at discovering such a detailed plot, of which he had hitherto had no more than a vague suspicion, prevailed over every other sentiment.

"It will be for Saturday," Verveuil repeated firmly, "unless further information obliges us to postpone the operation.... You're still resolved to help me to the end?"

"To the end."

"The men re-surfacing the building won't be working that day, since Malarche has decreed a national holiday. The owner of the house told me so anyway. They'll knock off the evening before, at six o'clock. That's when you'll have to take the rifle along. A woman attracts less attention. Dismantled, it doesn't take up much room and I've arranged for a package which won't be conspicuous, so don't worry."

"I'm not worrying."

"Good. I've already reconnoitred my line of withdrawal. After the operation you'll wait for me by the car some distance from the church. I'll let you know the exact spot later."

"You'll be alone? I mean, there won't be another marksman?"

Verveuil assumed the authoritative air of a born leader.

"My dear girl, I've already told you not to bother about what I have to do. Just follow my instructions and everything will be all right.... Yes, I'll be alone, if you must know," he added, changing his tone. "The committee have given me a free hand and the less people involved in this sort of business the better for all concerned. In fact as far as the practical side is concerned, there are only two of us, you and I, who know all the details. The owner of the house is only vaguely aware that something is being organised, and anyway the committee are getting him out of the country. He's leaving this very evening. . . . If there's a leak, it could only be through you or myself," he added, looking at her severely.

"You know you can count on me," she replied with a touch of contempt.

"I think so. . . . No point in our meeting too often between now and Saturday. Ring me up at the usual number if you have anything further to report. Meanwhile I'll let you have my latest instructions."

The conversation was over. Following the usual routine, Olga leapt to her feet with a scandalised expression, as though she had just received an improper suggestion, and hurried away. Verveuil waited a few moments, looking sheepish, then went off in another direction. In the truck, Martial Gaur carefully put the precious instrument back in its case and climbed into the driver's seat—which for him entailed a painful physical effort.

He drove slowly down the street. His leg hampered him, since the vehicle was not specially adapted for his use, but he scarcely noticed this, so absorbed was he by the thought of the plot which he had just discovered and in which he found himself so unexpectedly involved.

"The swine!" he muttered once more.

He repeated this insult several times under his breath, and now there was a note of indignation in his voice; but he was not sure himself whether he was inveighing against the conspirators because of their criminal intent or because they were using him as a dummy to obtain information.

"And that's not all," he growled again. "I'll have to notify the authorities."

He thought this over for some time, as though studying every aspect of the prospect, then spoke to himself again.

"I'll tell Herst all about it. That's the simplest solution. He's in a better position than anyone else to take the necessary action."

He happened to be not far from Herst's lodgings, which were likewise in the neighbourhood of the Luxembourg. For a moment he thought of stopping and alerting his friend at once.

He did not do so, however. He felt a strange inclination to examine every aspect of this affair more closely by himself. He went on driving, with no particular destination in view, engrossed in his own thoughts.

It was only after some time had elapsed that he noticed the route he was taking led straight to the church where the presidential wedding was to take place. He did not alter course when he realised this. A vague instinct prompted him to go and examine the spot more closely before deciding on what line of conduct to take.

9

HE WAS UNABLE TO PARK THE TRUCK near the church square and had to make his way there on foot. He arrived in a muck sweat, limping heavily, and only then noticed that he had walked far more quickly than was reasonable for him, though there was no apparent motive to justify such haste.

He sat down outside a café exactly opposite the church, ordered a drink which he did not touch, and remained for a long time as though in contemplation, gazing alternately at the expanse of the square and at a specific point on the church steps. In so doing, he was obeying a professional reflex.

A general view is what the photographer must seek to achieve first and foremost in the exercise of his profession. But this general picture did not prevent Martial from instinctively paying close attention to certain details whose importance cannot be overlooked by a conscientious camera operator. Thus he did not fail on this occasion to evaluate the intensity of the light, to check the position of the sun and to speculate on where it would be at the time of the ceremony.

After performing these routine operations almost unconsciously, he gave a shrug and pursed his lips, as though to say, "At a pinch it will do."

He left his glass untouched, rose to his feet and embarked on a slow circuit of the square, looking for the little street Verveuil and Olga had mentioned. It took him no time to find it; it was not far from the café where he had been sitting. He walked along it, stopping at frequent intervals to turn round and look behind him. One side of it was occupied by a blank wall without any openings. As for the other, because of the angle at which it ran, no window afforded a view of the church ... No window, but this did not apply to the scaffolding which Olga and Verveuil had mentioned and which he presently perceived himself. This jutted out appreciably in relation to the house fronts. From there the church steps were bound to be visible.

It gave Martial Gaur deep satisfaction to see for himself that the conspirators had not lied, that the plot was a reality and not a dream, a figment of his imagination, as he was still anxiously wondering only a moment before.

There were some men working on the scaffolding and the whole contraption was covered by a tarpaulin to hold back the dust. An excellent hiding-place for a marksman with criminal intent, he thought. Was it possible that the police had failed to notice this house? After a few moments' reflection Martial Gaur came to the conclusion that it was indeed quite possible, if not certain, as Olga claimed. Verveuil's plan seemed pretty sound. An odd reflex impelled him to speculate on its chances of success, his features tensed from concentration, as though this question was of prime importance to him.

He judged by eye the distance between the house and the church steps and reckoned it to be about a hundred yards. Verveuil had said eighty. Possibly: his own estimate was higher all the same. Verveuil was a good shot, admittedly, as Gaur was well aware, but maybe not as accurate as he claimed. At all events even a crack shot could not be absolutely certain of his aim at this range, considering his inevitable nervousness in the circumstances.

There was nothing else for him to look at in this street and he felt there was no point in hanging about any longer in the vicinity of the scaffolding, especially since Verveuil might quite possibly come prowling round to study the ground more closely. Pensively, he returned to the square and examined it with a fresh eye, with far greater attention than before, wrinkling his brow, racking his brains to imagine how it would look a few days later, at the moment the procession emerged from the church. Yet another powerful reflex of the photographer's is to form as accurate a mental image as possible of the final subject.

His face gradually clouded over as the picture took shape. The scene which now materialised in every detail afforded a very different aspect from that presented today by this relatively quiet square, an aspect sufficiently forbidding in his eyes to screw his features up into a painful grimace. What he saw, with a singular intensity, was the crowd, the appalling mob which was bound to conglomerate to witness such a spectacular event as this wedding. Thousands, tens of thousands of Parisians would be here, milling around, packed together like sardines, held back only with the greatest difficulty by police cordons.

He tried with visible anguish to imagine himself in the midst of this turmoil. Alas, he knew only too well it was a senseless effort. His disability forbade him such fantasies. All his recent experiences of crowds flashed across his memory to demonstrate the folly of his presence among such seething masses. With anguished eyes he continued to scan the expanse of the square in the feverish quest for some corner where he might find refuge, a corner from which he would have a view of the church steps without running the risk of being knocked over and trodden underfoot. He found none.

He clenched his fists as he visualised his colleagues drawn up in serried ranks right up in front. Jostled like the rest of the onlookers, but accustomed to such commotion, trained to sway to the surrounding eddies without ever taking their eyes off the target, alert as he himself once was, they always managed to take an exposure between one lurch and another. The magazines of the whole world would be sending the best men they had, all expert at catching the unusual element on the wing.

It was on this element, which no one was expecting, that his mind was now concentrated. He was too familiar with the reflexes and topical sense of press photographers to be unaware that dozens of cameras would rake the President like an almost instantaneous echo of the first rifle shot, again and again, several times in a few seconds. The outrage would not give rise to one outstanding document but to hundreds of unexceptional pictures, all of them more or less alike, among which the magazines would merely have to take their pick. As for himself, Martial Gaur, he would not even have the possibility of taking a single one in this series, commonplace though it might be by virtue of its sheer abundance.

There was nothing for him to do here. For a moment he deplored the instinct which had prompted him to come and explore this spot. On second thoughts, however, he did not regret this move since, now that he had reached a conclusion, he suddenly felt freed from the anxiety that had been preying on his mind ever since his discovery of the plot.

He shook his head vigorously, as though to get rid of his last remnant of doubt, and heard himself murmuring under his breath:

"I've waited too long already. It's time to warn the police. I must report this infamous scheme straight away."

73

10

HE WAS ABOUT TO LEAVE the square and return to his truck when, to his surprise, he caught sight of Herst standing motionless near the church steps. On second thoughts, he realised this was not so very astonishing. The bodyguard had probably likewise come to reconnoitre the ground and choose the spot where he would position himself with his men so as to keep the Head of State as closely as possible under surveillance while respecting his wishes to be left alone.

Herst had not seen him. Paradoxically, Martial's first reaction was to turn on his heels. Yet, struck by the absurdity of this attitude when only a minute before he had decided to go to his friend and tell him about his discovery, he remained where he was, though still unable to make up his mind to approach him.

He finally walked towards him only after several minutes' deep reflection, during which a plan spontaneously took shape in his mind, a plan that satisfied his wish to prevent this absurd outrage and at the same time his desire not to disrupt the natural course of events by an untimely act. It was a vague desire rooted in some obscure region of his mental universe, connected perhaps merely with his principle of impartiality and for which he would have been incapable, at this stage of the affair, of finding a reasonable motive.

Be that as it may, the ghost of a smile appeared on his lips when the outline of the plan materialised reasonably clearly in his mind's eye, and it was with perfect self-possession that he approached his friend.

"What the devil are you doing here?" Herst asked him.

Somewhat hypocritically, Martial Gaur assumed his most melancholy air in order to conceal the delight he felt at this moment at giving a personal impetus to events.

"Yes, you may well ask what the devil I'm doing here. I'm not up to this sort of work any longer."

Herst looked at him compassionately.

"I understand. You came to see if there was a possibility for you to take a photograph of the ceremony. . . . Some quiet spot . . . ."

"Don't be afraid of saying it—a spot where I'm not liable to get crushed or lose my remaining leg. But it's no good. I shan't even try."

"You might wangle yourself a place on one of those balconies."

Gaur shook his head with every sign of bitter melancholy.

"You know perfectly well there'll be as much commotion on the balconies as in the square itself. I shan't come, I tell you. A cripple, that's what I am. I'll console myself with my pin-ups, as usual."

Herst, who was a kindly man, felt extremely sorry

75

for him at this moment but, knowing him as he did, was careful not to show too much pity. He kept silent, not knowing what to say without further afflicting his friend. Martial Gaur took advantage of this silence and, glancing at him out of the corner of his eye with the expression of an angler casting his fly at a trout, went on:

"I apologise for being so grumpy, but I'm furious sometimes when I realise how handicapped I am . . . Just imagine, I had actually spotted a corner, admittedly rather far off, but where I should have been protected from the crowd. It's more than likely no one will think of it. But the snag is, you would have to be sound in wind and limb to reach this perch, be able to climb. And that's beyond me."

"An isolated perch no one will think of?" said Herst, with a swift change of expression. "Where did you discover this?"

"Are you interested?"

"Am I interested! Are you joking?"

"That's true. I keep forgetting your professional worries and I certainly wasn't thinking about security. Mind you, it's probably quite unimportant, but if you'd like to see for yourself, let's go down this street. . . . No, there's no need for that. You can see the place I mean from here. Look."

He led his friend up the church steps and made him stand in front of the door, on the very spot where the President would be.

"Over there."

"Good heavens!" Herst exclaimed with a sort of growl. "You're right."

76

He had noticed the edge of the scaffolding covered in a tarpaulin, which was perfectly visible from where he was standing.

"And no one spotted it!" he raged. "The inspectors assumed there was nothing to fear in that street."

"Sometimes the most obvious things escape us," Martial murmured. "I've often noticed that."

Then he added in a completely indifferent tone:

"Do you think there's any reason for keeping a watch on that house?"

"You can bet your life it will be kept under watch," the henchman thundered, taking a notebook from his pocket and starting to scribble furiously. "I'm extremely obliged to you, old man."

"Glad to have been of some use," said Gaur in the same tone.

"I'm going to do you a favour in return. . . . Yes, yes, I promise. An opportunity to take an outstanding snap of our dear President, if you're interested. Just you, nobody else, you watch!"

"Really?" said Martial, pricking up his ears.

"And maybe sooner than you think. I'll tell you about it later. . . . Just imagine, anyone in the world could have climbed up there and hidden away without our being any the wiser. That perch had escaped everyone's notice."

"It's my professional training," said Martial Gaur with a modest chuckle. "A photographer has to see everything. My eye's still fairly good even though I have a bad leg."

He turned away to conceal his satisfaction, while Herst went on taking notes. He had given an impetus to a certain train of events without yet knowing precisely where it would lead. But this was only the first step. He had to take another in order to maintain the momentum and there was no time to lose. An enquiry would no doubt be ordered and the house would be subjected to the strictest surveillance as from the very next day.

"By the way," he said to Herst. "I'm afraid I shan't be able to have dinner with you this evening. An urgent job on hand."

This evening he had to have a talk with Olga, in order to confine the events within the limits which his ingenious mind had fixed for the time being.

11

Sitting beside Olga in a little restaurant in Montparnasse, Gaur admired the girl's composure more than ever. Though the information he was giving her must be unleashing a storm in her brain, she appeared to attach no more importance to it than to a commonplace news item. He was also pretty satisfied with his own self-possession and the natural manner in which he had helped her to direct the conversation on to the subject they both had at heart. They were equally good actors. Their conversation was akin to a crafty fencing match and at times attained supreme artistry. It was he, however, who controlled the game.

The farce had started about seven o'clock when, having knocked on her door, he asked her in a pleasant and slightly bashful manner whether she was free to dine with him again that evening.

"You're beginning to make me lose my bachelor habits," he said with gruff affection.

He had started addressing her by the familiar *"tu"* the day before, with great diffidence, hesitating at times, playing the part of a surly old recluse who by degrees becomes domesticated, unconsciously and even unwillingly, and who feels disturbed by the thought that he is more infatuated than he realises.

"Darling, I think it's the same with me. . . ."

Bravo! She always produced the right retort. The impulse which flung her into his arms was a model of spontaneity.

"You're free?"

"For you, of course. Even if I weren't, I'd make arrangements."

He gazed at her in rapture.

"Darling! But you won't be angry if I have to leave you immediately afterwards? I have a union meeting at ten o'clock, which I can't miss."

"I'll make the best of a bad job. But didn't you tell me yesterday that you were dining with your friend Herst?"

She had a good memory where Herst was concerned. He did not fail to seize this opportunity of dropping a preliminary hint.

"I ran into him this afternoon and put him off. I so longed to see you again. . . . Anyway he's very busy these days. He hasn't a minute to spare. Just imagine, he has suddenly noticed there was an appalling flaw in the security plans for the President's wedding. Poor fellow! I'm sure he won't get much sleep tonight. I'll tell you all about it; it's terribly funny."

Having thus whetted her appetite, he admired her again for controlling her emotions completely except for a slight flutter of her eyelids. She asked him no questions and he dropped the subject for the time being.

"Will you give me half an hour to shave and get changed?"

"Half an hour, but not a minute longer. I'll come and fetch you."

Back in his own room, he turned the bath taps full on and slammed the bathroom door noisily, then crept back to listen without making a sound. He did not have long to wait. The murmur he presently heard did not surprise him. She was telephoning, she was warning Verveuil. Without being able to make out her words, he knew she was arranging a rendezvous with him for that evening. It was for this very purpose that he had made a point of telling her that he would have to leave her straight after dinner.

"Just imagine, poor old Herst . . ."

After he had ordered the meal with more than usual care, they had exchanged nothing but commonplace remarks for some time. He wondered with curiosity whether she would manage on her own to bring the conversation round to the burning question or whether he himself would be obliged to do so. It was she who opened fire, with a mastery he once again admired.

She placed her hand on his, darted him a glance overflowing with tenderness and said in an earnest manner:

"I must tell you. You don't know what pleasure you've given me by asking me out this evening instead of dining with your friend. But are you sure he isn't annoyed? I'd hate to think I was coming between the two of you in any way."

Not at all bad. At this moment he felt an almost genuine fondness for her and decided to help her forthwith.

"Darling, I assure you I wouldn't have hesitated to annoy him in order to be free this evening but, as I said before, I didn't have to. He's up to his eyes in work and has no time to eat. Just imagine . . ."

The course was set. He merely had to follow it.

"I felt like laughing, he looked so disconcerted. Just imagine, the poor fellow has been quaking in his shoes since this afternoon, and all on account of a scaffolding. . . ."

"On account of a scaffolding?"

A slightly breathless note had crept into her voice all the same and he felt her fingers tremble. He pretended not to notice.

"Yes, a scaffolding. I couldn't quite understand what it was all about—something to do with angles of view, as far as I could gather. To cut a long story short, he had gone to have a look at the church where the presidential wedding is to take place. . . . I told you about his fears, you remember? Well, although several people responsible for security had already reconnoitred the square, Herst, who has a quick eye, noticed that a certain scaffolding—in a side-street, I believe—had completely escaped the inspectors' notice, though it affords an ideal position for a possible killer. At this moment Herst must be busy warning all the authorities to have the house kept under watch, enquire into its occupants and so forth. Funny they never spotted it before, don't you think?"

She did not reply straight away. She had turned her

82

head slightly. She looked at him again after a moment or two and remarked in an indifferent tone:

"I don't suppose it's funny for your friend. But has he any real reason for believing an attempt will be made on the life of the Head of State? In this day and age, it seems fantastic."

The conversation was taking a turn which served his plan of action perfectly. He was careful not to let her veer off the subject and replied dubiously:

"That's what I've often asked myself. Admittedly, there are always fanatics and lunatics to contend with. But I think Herst is suffering somewhat from a professional idiosyncrasy. If you ask me, it would need someone who was both a lunatic and a fanatic to make an attempt during a ceremony like next week's."

"Do you think so?"

"Work it out yourself. Every security department has been mobilised, and even if they happen to overlook a detail like the scaffolding it's hardly likely that an assassin could bring it off. And even if he did, he would have no chance of escaping from the police. Arrangements have been made for cordoning off the whole neighbourhood at a moment's notice."

"Really?"

"At least that's what Herst told me," he casually said, "and he's certainly better informed than anyone else."

A long silence ensued. The subject, a trivial one on the whole, seemed to be exhausted and neither of them appeared to want to discuss it any further. In actual fact Martial Gaur was thinking of the next remark he was going to make, a trite statement that seemed calculated to wind up the futile topic once and for all, a statement which he did not for the moment consider of vital importance but which he intuitively felt was a necessary stone in the edifice that was beginning to take shape in his subconscious.

He therefore took great care to interject this remark between two fairly long silences, as a virtuoso isolates a series of brilliant notes in order to emphasise them. This in no way detracted—rather the reverse, in fact—from the perfectly natural tone and air of complete detachment with which he went on:

". . . Whereas in the case of a President like Pierre Malarche, who's well known for flouting the conventions of the Elysée and reducing his bodyguards to despair through his spirit of independence, there would be far easier and less dangerous opportunities available to a criminal. . . ."

12

THE WEDDING TOOK PLACE without mishap. Thousands of photographs were taken of the President as he came out of the church with his young bride on his arm, but they were more or less identical and totally devoid of the unusual quality without which they had no appeal for an aesthete like Gaur. He had not even bothered to leave his room, and merely followed the ceremony on his television set. He had good reason to believe that there would be no disturbance, but was nevertheless profoundly relieved when the ceremony came to an end. The President was safe and would probably never know the risk he had run.

There was someone else who felt a great weight lifted from his shoulders when Pierre Malarche left the church and especially when he finally withdrew to his private residence at the end of the day. Herst rang Martial up less than a quarter of an hour after coming off duty.

"Well, how did it go?"

"Whew! Thank God it's over!"

"Really?"

"You can't imagine what a relief it is. Everything went off perfectly. Now I'm going to have at least two weeks' peace and quiet, because he won't be appearing in public for some time. I'd like to see you. I may have an interesting proposition for you, and above all I want to thank you."

"Thank me?"

"Yes. It seems there actually was something fishy about that house with the scaffolding."

"What!"

"I'll tell you when I see you."

They arranged to meet in the bar. As soon as Martial arrived, Herst, who had already drained his glass, led him into the quiet corner where he had chosen a table.

"The drinks are on me today," he said. "That's the least I owe you. Do you know your photographer's eye probably did us a great service? That house you spotted was suspect."

"You don't say!"

This gave no pleasure to Martial Gaur, who even felt extremely annoyed. He had no wish for the suspects to be arrested and it was with deep misgiving that he asked for further details.

"The owner of the house in question wriggled out of our investigation. He has mysteriously disappeared and there's every reason to believe that he's fled abroad. What's more, it seems certain that he belonged to a seditious group. A strange coincidence, don't you think?"

"Maybe. Nothing more definite in the way of clues?"

86

"The police are pursuing their enquiries. They haven't yet finished, as far as I know."

Gaur drained his glass in one gulp, fell silent for a moment, then went on:

"What else? You said you had a proposition to make to me."

"I think you'll find it interesting. You remember that time Malarche went for a ride alone in the forest?"

"Of course. Thanks again for tipping me off."

"Well, I hope to be able to give you another tip of the same sort soon."

"As good as that?"

"Even better."

Martial's heart started beating violently.

"Better? You're a real friend, old boy. If you do this for me . . ."

"Nonsense. You've earned it, I tell you."

The tip to which Herst had just referred had been an absolute godsend to the photographer. It concerned one particular occasion when Pierre Malarche went for a ride all by himself—the sort of escapade in which he liked to indulge from time to time, to the despair of his bodyguard. Herst, who acted more or less as his confidant in this sort of affair, had told Gaur about it the day before, knowing that the latter would hold his tongue, being only too happy to exploit this exclusive information. Concealed in a thicket, Martial was able to take a pretty remarkable photograph which eventually appeared on the front page of a weekly magazine. Malarche had blindly believed it was the work of an amateur and had taken no offence. He was keen on his reputation as a sportsman and man of independent spirit. He did not mind evidence of this being published, seeing that he had not been bothered at all in the process.

Herst could obviously not repeat this friendly gesture very often, for fear of rendering his own discretion suspect. But from time to time it was possible.

"I remember now. You mentioned something of the sort the day we met outside the church."

"I thought it was the best way to raise your spirits. Well, it's taking shape. You know the President is shortly going on a long tour which will take him to the south of France and in particular the Mediterranean coast, which is where he comes from?"

"I heard something about it."

"An official tour, but at the same time a sort of honeymoon. He and his better half want to take advantage of this to have a few days' holiday, which in his case means being able to breathe freely, walk about where he likes, go for a swim perhaps—she loves the sea and so does he—without the constant presence of an official retinue and above all without having a gang of thugs like Uncle Herst and his henchmen breathing down his neck."

"I don't blame him."

"Nor do I, as a matter of fact. But that's not the point. Since he has to have an accomplice to achieve this freedom, he has already instructed me to engineer some escapades of this sort for him. Yes, I'm now the organiser of his clandestine leisure hours. It's enough to turn one's hair grey! So if you have nothing better to do, and if you happen to be on the spot when he takes it into his head to play truant, I'm practically certain of being able to give you another interesting tip. . . . I'm your friend after all, aren't I? "

"A real friend, as I said before."

Martial Gaur clasped his hand with an emotion that was anything but feigned. Good old Herst! Ever since they had known each other, back in the Resistance days, he had never failed to do his best and let him know whenever there was something worthy of interest to a photographer.

"Don't worry. I'll follow the tour and keep in touch with you. You have no idea what such an opportunity means to me. I feel I'm living again and am no longer a cripple."

Herst shrugged his shoulders.

"If I'm in your debt over that scaffolding business, Malarche is even more so. I'm pretty well convinced that he owes you a great deal, maybe even his life. It's only fair he should show his gratitude, even indirectly."

"Yes, that's true," Martial replied pensively.

89

13

HE WOKE WITH A SLIGHT HEADACHE, having parted company with his friend fairly late the night before after drinking more than usual. Both of them were in the state of euphoria that demands some outside stimulus: Herst because he was rid of his responsibilities and anxieties for a while, Gaur because he felt that events were taking a satisfactory turn after the slight impetus he had given them.

He ordered some coffee, drank two cups while thinking of Herst's promises and at once felt clear-headed and sharp-eyed, so alert that as soon as he got up he noticed a detail that had escaped him the day before: the fourth wire, the microphone wire, had disappeared. He verified that the instrument itself was no longer there. A few scratches on the paintwork were the only evidence of Olga's eavesdropping.

The discovery irritated him at first, then his face lighted up. Olga had obviously felt that their relationship now made such cloak-and-dagger accessories superfluous. They were even dangerous, for their fortuitous discovery could compromise a situation that was now well-established on both sides. She was absolutely right. He decided to take the same precaution and go round that very morning to return the ultra-directional microphone which Tournette had lent him several days before and which he had since kept hidden away in one of his suitcases.

There was another reason which prompted him to contact his old friend whom he still regarded as his master. Up to now he had acted intuitively and under the pressure of events. Today he felt uncertain as to his future line of conduct, as to the opportunity of making a deeper imprint on the web of destiny and as to the direction in which this eventual step was to be taken. There was no question of course of asking Tournette's advice. Martial Gaur never asked anyone for advice, not even his mentor, and in any case he would have been at a loss to give a clear definition of the problem that was still thrashing about in his subconscious. But the mere company of the old fellow, and the views he never failed to voice, might possibly enlighten him. Even the strongest personalities sometimes feel the need for a mutual exchange of ideas.

When he arrived, Tournette was in the process of photographing a flower, a rose he had selected from a bunch of others, which would not have attracted the notice of a layman but in which he himself discerned a particular movement of the petals. Gaur knew he was not to be disturbed when he was absorbed by this sort of work. He sat down silently in a corner of the room and observed his friend with a smile. To him it was a pleasure and at the same time an intellectual recreation to watch him operate. Tournette was probably the only human being he really admired and in whose presence he felt like an apprentice in the presence of his master.

Half blind (in order to work he used a dozen different pairs of spectacles and kept cursing and complaining that he still did not have a sufficient number to give him a complete range of vision), the old man never left his room, spending all his time stirring up old memories, examining his collections and occasionally, as was the case this morning, taking an exposure for his own personal pleasure. At one time he had been famous as a press photographer, but now he was practically forgotten and lived like a hermit. Gaur was the only person who called on him at more or less regular intervals.

Tournette was absorbed for the moment by the arrangement of his subject. He kept changing the position of the rose. He added a little water to the vase, then, having stepped back and changed his spectacles, poured it away again with a gesture of exasperation. After remaining for some time in contemplation, he rushed over to the window and adjusted the height of the blinds several times. Then he shifted the screen and consulted various optical instruments, some of which were unfamiliar even to Gaur himself. He looked perplexed and pulled a face which accentuated his many wrinkles. Picking up a view-finder, he squinted through it from various angles but appeared unable to find a suitable one. He tried, apparently with equal lack of success, standing on a stool, then dropping down on all fours, having to stop several times to get his breath, taking advantage of these pauses to change a colour filter, consult various other instruments or yet again modify the lighting which clearly did not satisfy him.

All the time he was moving about like this, he was not silent but in his quavering voice kept uttering short, unrelated sentences which were often quotations from the works of French or foreign authorities on photography, of which he possessed a fairly complete collection. This idiosyncrasy, which had grown more pronounced in his old age, sometimes irritated Gaur, but today he listened to him with particular attention.

"In a perfect photograph there will be as many beauties lurking unobserved as there are flowers that blush unseen in forests and meadows."

"Who said that?"

"Oliver Wendell Holmes. 1859. One of the first men to have glimpsed the possibilities of photography."

He bustled about again, changed his spectacles, then paused for a moment.

"But Holmes didn't see everything. He didn't even see the main point. The art of allowing details to emerge which the eye generally fails to see in nature. . . . I quite agree. There's another saying—the photographer must visualise in advance the general construction of his picture . . . But seeing or foreseeing isn't enough, even a good amateur can manage that without much effort. The main point for us, Gaur is to create. To *create*, do you hear? That's something no one understood in the old days and which many haven't yet understood. It's not a question of slavish recording. . . . I don't like the term 'photographer'. It's pejorative. The photographer must be a creator in the same way as the painter. I know what you're going to say. . . ."

"I'm going to say, of course, that it's often impossible."

"Impossible!" the old man exclaimed indignantly.

Gaur knew these arguments of his by heart but took pleasure in egging him on and arousing his enthusiasm.

"It's easy for you these days, and also for me to a certain extent. But it's impossible for the press photographer who has to seize on an event, which for the most part is unforeseeable, instantaneously. It's quite a feat for him even to record it faithfully."

"That's not true," old Tournette growled. "We always, always, do you hear—even for impromptu pictures—we always have the possibility of transposing, transcending reality. That's what distinguishes the artist from the good artisan. That's why I ...."

He interrupted his work irritably, closed the window and put away his instruments.

"Impossible today," he muttered. "The light's no good. I'll try again tomorrow. . . . I was saying the artist worthy of the name must make his personal imprint even on the most transitory image. You don't believe me? Listen. You know my photograph of Sandra?"

Martial Gaur pricked up his ears. This photograph had once been widely acclaimed and was still discussed in professional circles even though its author had lapsed into oblivion. It had roused the jealousy of every camera operator of Tournette's generation.

Sandra was one of the most famous international cinema actresses, celebrated for her beauty, her talent and her love affairs. At the height of her glory, even slightly past her prime perhaps, she had apparently been seized by a fit of madness, had climbed up on to the roof of a large house she had rented for a visit to Paris and committed suicide by flinging herself into the street, after several minutes' hesitation, thus enabling a large number of onlookers to gather on the pavement below.

Tournette, who was hanging about the building waiting for the star's appearance, happened to be in the forefront of the crowd. It was then that he took the famous photograph, a document which was considered exceptional on account of the extraordinary expression on the subject's face. Sandra died a few moments later.

"Didn't you ever wonder about that expression which I had the good fortune to catch? Didn't you ever ask yourself to what it was due?"

"Largely a matter of luck, I suppose. It was chance that took you to that particular spot in the street and enabled you to record the look in her eyes as she lay dying."

"My dear boy! Luck? Chance? As far as my presence in the street at the right moment is concerned, yes, perhaps; although I myself prefer to call it flair. But that by itself isn't enough. Other people also have luck. Other people might have recorded the expression on the dying actress's face, but it wouldn't have been the *same* expression, don't you see?"

A strange gleam had come into the old man's eyes. He was elated by the memory of his success and went on with rather solemn emotion:

"That expression, which gave the picture whatever value it had, which caused it to be reproduced all over the world . . ."

He was not exaggerating. Sandra's dying expression exuded an almost supernatural radiance, an hallucinating mixture of anguish, suffering and despair, one of those mysterious emanations which leave a deep impression on the public, on simple and sophisticated souls alike, which provoke a fever of excitement among magazine owners, causing them to indulge in extravagant gestures, prompting them to pick up the telephone with a trembling hand and order an editor to change the make-up of an almost completed issue at the very last moment, to cut out no matter what, to modify the lay-out of every page from top to bottom, if necessary, so as to be able to print the sublime document on the cover. Martial Gaur had never achieved such a triumph.

"It was I who provoked that expression," Tournette went on in the same tone. "Without me it would never have existed. I created it. Thanks to me, Armand Tournette, a merely original picture became unique, sensational."

He lowered his voice slightly, as though deeply moved by these recollections, and continued in a dull tone, while Martial never took his eyes off him.

"When I went up to the body, I found myself confronted with an expressionless face, frozen by shock. My camera was ready. I took an initial picture, of course, but of no great value. I never published it. The features were lifeless, as I said.

"It was while reloading my camera, still examining the face intently, that I noticed a fluttering of the eyelids, no doubt a reflex caused by the click of the shutter release. The onlookers were terrified and dared

96

not come close. I, on the other hand, kept my head. I went on observing and reflecting, breathless with suspense, as you can well imagine. I realised she was not completely unconscious and I saw a glimmer of hope."

"Yes, there was still a slight hope perhaps," said Martial, continuing to look at him intently. "What did you do then?"

"I had an inspiration," said the old photographer, unable to conceal the pride he felt at evoking this exploit of his youth, "an intuition, one of those flashes that illuminate an artist's life and for which I have often thanked the powers that be.

"Like everyone else, I knew about Sandra's love affairs and in particular her latest, with a young man barely emerged from his 'teens who, according to rumour, was on the point of leaving her for a much younger actress. This girl's star was just beginning to rise, whereas Sandra's was on the decline. . . . A heaven-sent inspiration, I tell you! Only twice in my life have I ever felt anything approaching it. I placed myself in the best position. I focused my camera on her, with my finger poised on the shutter release, and pronounced out loud the name of her rival and that of her faithless lover.

"At that moment, Martial, she opened her eyes. At that moment I was able to fix for eternity her expression of despair. Not a single aspect of it was missed. It wasn't a question of luck or chance. The look in her eyes was the very look I had wanted.

"After that I rushed off. I ran all the way home. I was in torment until I had developed the film. I was afraid something might have gone wrong. But my fears were groundless. The exposure was perfect."

Old Tournette had come to the end of his story, and in the ensuing silence Martial started poring over his own memories. He reflected bitterly that though he had often had occasion to catch the look in a dying man's eyes, never, alas, had he had such a stroke of luck as his friend—luck or, as the latter seemed to believe, genius. For a moment it occurred to him that their conversation was not that of two normal human beings and that if a third person had happened to overhear it he would probably have been utterly appalled. As though reading his thoughts, the old man uttered one of his usual sayings by way of conclusion:

"The photographer is an artist. The artist must be capable of being inhuman."

Martial went on sitting in his chair without saying a word. His old master appeared to him like a denizen of a distant planet, despatched to ours by members of some superior civilisation and entrusted with the mission of making a pictorial record of the customs and behaviour of the strange creatures inhabiting this earth.

He was roused from his reverie by a question from Tournette, who asked him if the ultra-directional microphone had been of any use to him.

"Extremely useful, yes," he replied absently. "Thanks very much. It worked perfectly and I didn't miss a single word of the conversation in which I was interested."

"And you think it's going to enable you to take a valuable picture?"

This was the pretext he had given when borrowing the instrument. He began to reply in the same absent tone:

"Very likely. I . . ."

He broke off all of a sudden, as though a blazing light had just dazzled him. The disjointed and embryonic fragments of thoughts that had been whirling through his brain for the last few days suddenly seemed to fall into a compact and coherent whole. He went on in an unusually vehement tone which made old Tournette raise his head and peer at him in surprise over his spectacles, discerning in his remark a singularly youthful note, like an echo of his former enthusiasm:

"One never can tell."

14

"DARLING, I HAVE something to ask you."

Olga and Martial Gaur, who had been to see an
avant-garde play at a theatre in the Latin Quarter, were
walking back to their hotel, choosing deserted little
side-streets. They had both been strangely silent during
the evening. Martial was so pensive that he had not
realised that his girl friend was even less expansive
than usual. They had discussed commonplace topics
and, after the show, had exchanged no more than a few
vague opinions on the play they had just seen, the plot
of which he would have been quite incapable of des-
cribing, so absorbed had he been by his own thoughts.

It was this very evening that he had decided to give
another impetus to the train of events in which destiny
had involved him. This second step had to be taken
without delay and, now that he was about to take the
plunge, he felt not exactly a qualm but the sense of
uneasiness that assails one at the moment of committing oneself completely to an undertaking and consci-
ously picking up the reins that have hitherto been left
dangling at random.

This vague sensation evaporated shortly after coming out of the theatre and he delayed no longer in giving the necessary boost to implement his project, a plan that had suddenly escaped from the realm of the subconscious and was assuming a more and more definite shape in his mind.

All that was needed, as a matter of fact, was a slight boost. He gave it with his usual adroitness, after composing his features like an expert actor.

"Darling, I have something to ask you."

"And I have something to tell you."

He was so immersed in his role that he hardly noticed Olga's reply.

"Please, let me speak first. . . . This is the situation: I'll be going on a journey shortly. . . . Oh, not far, down south. For a fortnight probably. Rather a pleasant jaunt, in fact, a sort of busman's holiday, which will no doubt take me to the Mediterranean coast."

"You're going to leave me?"

"That's what I'm worrying about. That's why I haven't dared mention it before. Listen, I have no wish to lie to you, even in the smallest way. You know how I love my freedom. So I may as well tell you straight away: yes, I was thinking of going off on my own."

"No need to apologise. I understand perfectly. I've told you a thousand times."

"Yes, you're marvellous. But today . . . this evening, for quite some time in fact, I've found I'm wretched whenever I'm away from you. I may as well admit it: I've never felt like this before."

What could she say in reply? She squeezed his hand and murmured:

101

"I feel exactly the same."

An expression of joy, admirably contrived, lighted up Martial's face.

"Really? Then I'll be brave. I wanted to ask you if you could come with me."

He had placed his hand on her shoulder, stopping to ask her this favour which sounded almost like a prayer. Her shoulder gave a slight twitch, the only sign of vexation which this invitation must have caused her. It was obvious she was pondering on something quite different from a trip to the south with her lover.

"Darling! You really mean it? You thought of taking me with you? I'd love to! But there's my job to consider," she went on in a tone akin to despair.

"That's true," he muttered with an air of disappointment. "I was so delighted at the prospect of this trip that I'd forgotten your work. Can't you give up the shop for a little while?"

"When are you leaving?"

"In two weeks or so. You see, it doesn't depend on me. I'll know the exact date shortly."

She assumed a solemn air, nodded her head and appeared to give the matter deep thought.

"Can't you postpone this journey till a little later? To give me time to make arrangements?"

"Alas! The date doesn't depend on me, as I said."

He burst out laughing and assumed a mirthful expression.

"Believe it or not, my journey is closely connected with the movements of the President of the Republic."

He derived a subtle pleasure from playing this cat-and-mouse game with her. He did not even need to look at her face to sense the emotion aroused in her by this new aspect of the question.

"It's the result of a promise from dear old Herst, whom I shouldn't make fun of as I sometimes do, for he's the best friend a man could have. It would be stupid of me to miss such an opportunity."

He repeated to her everything Herst had told him about the escapades Pierre Malarche was planning and of his promise to enable him to take a unique photograph of the Head of State playing truant.

"You see," he concluded, "for someone in my state, a godsend like this occurs once in a lifetime."

To put the finishing touches to the role he was playing, he assumed a forlorn manner, as he had done with Herst.

"I sometimes feel such a cripple. Struck off the list of a corporation of which I was once the head. You don't know what it's like."

"Darling!"

She embraced him with a touching spontaneity. He pretended to wipe his eyes and held her at arm's length, shaking his head vigorously.

"But I realise you can't leave your shop. It would be too selfish of me. I'll be thinking of you every day, I promise."

She pressed up against him again and appeared to take a great decision.

"Listen. I'm going to do everything I can. There's a friend of mine who usually takes my place when I'm away on holiday. I'll ring her up tomorrow."

"You really will?"

"Can't you see I long for this trip even more than

you do?" she exclaimed, flinging her arms round his neck and kissing him passionately. "Besides, I believe in hunches. Something tells me I'll bring you luck, that I must be with you, and then you'll get a really sensational photograph."

"I'm sure of it," he said, returning her kiss.

They walked the rest of the way to their hotel hand in hand. It was now Olga's turn to be absorbed and silent. She opened her mouth several times as though she was about to say something, then thought better of it. She made up her mind only after a great deal of hesitation.

"Darling, I said just now that I had something to tell you."

He raised his head in surprise. His own manoeuvres had made him forget this statement of hers.

"Something to tell me?"

"Something serious. And I must tell you this evening. I must tell you before we go on this trip, which may bring us even closer together. I have no right to go on lying to you, to pretend to be what I'm not. It's not an easy confession to make, but it's necessary...."

A confession? This was not at all to Martial Gaur's liking. What was biting her? Was she going to ruin everything? Seized by sudden incomprehensible scruples, was she going to destroy in a second the beautiful simplicity of his plan?

"It's like this. Poulain isn't my real name and I'm not the country girl that you imagine."

One night she had told him a story about her parents dying in poverty, in consequence of which she had

104

been obliged to come to Paris to earn her living. He
had listened to her without paying much attention. He
knew perfectly well, of course, that this was all pure
invention. He also suspected that she had assumed a
fictitious name. He was shrewd enough to see through
her character without any help from her. Was she
going to make a full confession which would confront
him with an unbearable alternative: denouncing her
or becoming her accomplice? This would completely
upset his strategy, which was simple, and he considered simplicity the greatest virtue of all. He had to
prevent this at all costs.

"I don't care about your name, darling, still less
about your past life. I'm not asking you anything."

"Yes, but I want you to know exactly what you
ought to know about me and my background."

There was no stopping her! Furious at her persistence, he again attempted to stop her, but she went on
in the authoritative manner which she was capable of
assuming on certain occasions.

"I must. My real name is Olga Jardan. Jardan, does
that mean anything to you? I can see it does."

It did not require a great effort of memory for him to
recall this name, which had appeared on the front page
of every daily paper the year before.

"Jardan? You mean Pierre Jardan, the . . ."

"The gangster. Pierre Jardan, known as Pierrot le
Bourgeois," she said in a dull voice. "I'm his daughter.
I had to tell you, even if it means losing you for
ever."

They had arrived outside their hotel. He stopped a
few yards from the entrance and looked at her in

silence, peering into her face, every feature of which was visible in the light from the windows of the bar.

Pierre Jardan was a gangster of the old school. Martial had read his story out of curiosity. He remembered now that there had been some mention of a daughter, and her photograph had actually been published in one paper. Here at last was the explanation of his impression that he had seen Olga's face somewhere before. At the time of the trial this girl had appeared as one of the few factors in favour of Jardan, which his lawyer had attempted in vain to exploit. He had always kept her apart from his criminal life and had given her a good education.

The whole of the gangster's history now came back to him. Pierre Jardan, known as le Bourgeois, had eluded the police for a long time. After bringing off several fruitful jobs, he had lain low for a number of years, leading the peaceful life of a pensioner, hence his nickname. Then, impelled by nostalgia or the need for money, he had attempted one last exploit, which proved fatal to him.

He had shot and mortally wounded a police inspector in the course of a hold-up. His trial gave rise to rather heated arguments in court, Jardan maintaining that he had fired in the air and that the killing was the work of an accomplice who had taken flight. There was some probability in this claim but, coming on top of so many similar crimes in which the culprit had escaped justice, the murder of a policeman could not go unpunished. Jardan was therefore condemned to death.

He had been executed a few months previously, his appeal having failed ... Good heavens! Martial Gaur felt dizzy for a moment. The gangster's appeal had been refused by the Head of State! The Head of State was then Pierre Malarche, who had just been elected. He suddenly realised the motives that dictated Olga's conduct: hatred and thirst for revenge.

He felt vaguely relieved at this discovery. These were motives which he was able to understand and acknowledge. For some time he had felt, if not love, a genuine fondness for his mistress. He admired her intelligence and was pleased she had not sunk so low as to allow herself to be guided by the wretched political motives of a puppet like Verveuil, which would have made him despise her.

He did not even have to force himself to clasp her hand more firmly, with the sort of friendly understanding that no woman can resist.

"Is that all? Is that your serious confession?"

Yes, that was all. He breathed more freely than he had done for several minutes. That was all; she had never contemplated going any further. So much the better.

"I tell you again and you must believe me. What you have just said makes absolutely no difference to our relationship. Your past life doesn't interest me in the least, nor does your father's."

She flung herself into his arms and pressed her tear-stained face against his.

"You're the best man in the world. My past life horrifies me and I'd give anything to forget it. Since knowing you, I almost have."

She excelled, as he did, in mingling truth with false-hood, so craftily that her lies sounded like genuine

107

statements of fact. This confession she had just made, which could easily be checked and was therefore not open to doubt, was further evidence of her supreme ability. He had told her once that he felt he had seen her face somewhere before. This must have given her food for thought: if he had discovered her real identity off his own bat, she would have appeared suspect to him at once. She had averted this risk by an ingenuous avowal.

"Let's not ever mention it again," he said.

They went into the hotel. He urged her to spend the whole night with him in his room, which was contrary to their habits. She agreed, all the more joyfully, she said as she lay down beside him, that for the next few days she would probably not be able to see him as often as she wished.

"I'll be very busy making all the arrangements for my departure and handing over to the girl who's going to relieve me. . . . Because it's decided, darling, I'm coming with you. Nothing could stop me. It'll be a marvellous holiday."

While he embraced her with the ardour of a lover who is oblivious of the rest of the world and for whom nothing matters except his passion for his mistress as soon as she opens her arms to him, he reflected that he had been quite right to return Tournette's indiscreet instrument.

There was no further need for them to eavesdrop on each other. It was utterly pointless for him to listen in to the conversations she would have with Verveuil in the course of the next few days. For this certainly was the reason why she wanted to be left free. They would have little more than a fortnight to draw up fresh plans.

Utterly pointless indeed. From now on he himself would be suggesting to them whatever steps they were to take, and the remarks they exchanged would be merely the echo of the information he casually passed on to Olga. The intoxicating thought that he was now directing events as he pleased gave additional spice to every embrace that night and it was with a proud feeling of domination, oddly mingled with the satisfaction of his senses, that, after prolonging their amatory dalliance to an unusual degree, he fell asleep exhausted in his mistress's arms.

Part Two

Part Two

1

Président Pierre Malarche was proceeding on his tour, accompanied by his young wife, flanked by his bodyguards, surrounded by his official retinue, unaware that he was also drawing in his wake a clandestine escort of individuals who took no interest in the receptions and speeches but were inspired by violent feelings and a fierce singleness of purpose. For Martial Gaur this was a period of great intensity, alternating between hope and anxiety, which recalled the finest days of his adventurous youth. He felt giddy at the thought that in his hands alone were assembled all the threads of a web of delicate intrigue. He saw himself as a sort of demiurge commanding a confused chaos of elements and directing them towards a creation whose advent no one but himself could foresee.

He had left by car with Olga, preceding or following the presidential procession by several hours so as to avoid the crowds, but taking care not to lose contact for too long, for fear of something happening in his absence. Olga seemed to like this programme and they would smile at each other from time to time for no apparent reason, gazing at each other like two lovers for whom the hazards of travel are a source of perpetual delight and afford endless opportunities for an upsurge of affection. At certain times the pleasure Martial felt in his mistress's company made him look upon this jaunt as a happy combination of professional assignment and pleasure cruise, much the same sort of combination as the presidential tour itself.

His pleasure did not, however, make him forget the main purpose of the expedition, but his hour had not yet come. He occasionally took some long-distance views of an official reception, simply to keep his eye in. These pictures were of no value. The local photographers occupied the best places. It was only in the south that he himself would find the opportunity of operating to the full. Herst had told him so—Herst who was once again worried to death and overworked and who, at the end of the day, would sometimes come and have a drink with his friend to relax and forget his worries.

Martial, however, had taken care not to tell the henchman of his relationship with Olga or even of her existence. They always took separate rooms in the hotels at which they stayed.

"You see, the information he has given me is absolutely confidential. He wouldn't trust me if he knew there was a woman in my life."

"Of course, I understand. I'd never forgive myself if you missed this opportunity because of me."

For greater security, they had decided to sleep in their respective rooms. He asked her with a sigh to share this sacrifice.

114

"Herst thinks I'm on my own. He can drop in and see me at any time of the day."

She had conceded with an even more harrowing sigh than his own, concealing the satisfaction she felt at this solution. There was of course another reason, at least as important as the first, why he was anxious to leave her absolutely free. Did she not need a free hand to communicate with Verveuil? Verveuil had to be informed straight away of all the information Herst might give him. This had already happened at the beginning of the trip, when the President had expressed his desire to go for a walk some time by himself. On that occasion Gaur, after telling Olga about it, excused himself on the grounds of a headache and went to bed early, falling asleep reassured only after hearing her furtively open the door of her room and go out to a nocturnal rendezvous. But the project had been cancelled on the following day and he made a point of informing them of this at once.

The photographer's punctilious mind overlooked not a single detail. He never failed to tell Olga at which hotel they would be staying and the numbers of the rooms he had booked, so as to facilitate contact between the conspirators even further. He was delighted when one day he realised that, as he had hoped, the two accomplices had found a less dangerous means of communication than the telephone, which by this time was causing him some anxiety on their behalf. It was not long before he perceived, in fact, that the left-hand shutter in Olga's bedroom was drawn back when he had decided to spend the evening with her, whereas it was the other shutter when he was due to leave her early. The somewhat childish satisfaction he derived from this discovery helped to beguile his impatience.

For Verveuil was part of Pierre Malarche's clandestine following—of this Martial Gaur was as certain as if he had seen him with his own eyes, just as he knew exactly what his state of mind must be. Though Verveuil regarded himself as a superior being sent by Destiny to change the course of history, Martial saw him as a mere puppet in his own hands.

What part did Olga herself play in this business? Another puppet whose strings he was manipulating? Certainly. He considered her infinitely superior, however, to her wretched acolyte whose orders she pretended to accept but whom she too was actually using like a mindless robot. She was manipulating him in more or less the same way as he himself was, exploiting his fanaticism and stupidity to wreak her own revenge: a purpose of which he neither approved nor disapproved but which he considered to be in a far higher intellectual class than Verveuil's ridiculous political motives. He admired her more and more. Occasionally he even felt a sort of spiritual communion with her, the fraternity of higher minds which rise above the petty concerns of the general run of mankind.

Ever since she had revealed her identity to him, he no longer had any uncertainty as to her role. He still had a faint doubt, however, as to the motive which had prompted her to admit she was Jardan's daughter. Had she done so with cunning foresight or in a moment of weakness? It was a problem which disturbed him at times. Was she still on her guard or did she, as she lay beside him, sometimes feel an urge to be frank? He came to the conclusion that the latter hypothesis was not at all likely.

He sometimes also wondered if she was completely taken in by the part he himself was playing or whether she did not regard him rather as an accomplice who had drawn up a tacit agreement with her. But this doubt always evaporated after a few moments' reflection and he decided with pride that it was utterly out of the question. His own game could not be apprehended by any being on earth or in heaven. Tournette perhaps, Tournette, at a pinch, might have been capable of seeing through it; but Tournette could in no way be regarded as a terrestrial creature, still less as a celestial spirit.

2

AMONG MARTIAL'S ANXIETIES, which sometimes disturbed the serenity of the journey, first and foremost was Verveuil's security, one of the essential factors of his plan. Knowing the man's stupidity, he was occasionally haunted by the fear of seeing him commit some blunder which would bring him to the notice of the police.

Herst accentuated his anxiety on this score one evening when, after coming off duty, he had met him in a café in Valence where the President had stopped for the night. The henchman looked gloomy and careworn. When Gaur asked him if he had something on his mind, he gave an impatient shrug.

"Always the same worry, and it will go on as long as this journey lasts, as long as Malarche continues to flaunt himself in public every day. At the moment we're all on tenterhooks because of that scaffolding business . . . the outcome of that business, rather."

"What!" Martial exclaimed, pricking up his ears. "Did the investigation lead to something?"

"Not to the arrest of any culprits or suspects. But as

far as I can gather—because I haven't been put in the picture completely—it has brought to light a number of disturbing facts. The owner of the house never reappeared and it's now certain he was on the payroll of an extremely dangerous subversive organisation. I'm told there's evidence of a proposed attempt on the President's life on his wedding day, a plan that was cancelled when the police started investigating the house. . . . But it may only have been postponed."

"Have any names come to light?" Gaur enquired, without appearing to attach any importance to his question.

"I wouldn't be surprised. All I know is that we've been ordered to keep a closer watch, and as from to-morrow the police are going to carry out a thorough check on every hotel in every town where the President is due to stop. Every traveller who can't account for himself, or whose presence doesn't appear to be justified, will be subject to a very strict surveillance. The security measures will even include snap searches of the luggage of men travelling by themselves."

"Men travelling by themselves?"

"As I said before, I don't know the details, but it seems the branch in charge of the investigation came across some clues which suggest that the danger might come from a lone killer."

This made the photographer's blood run cold. Excusing himself on the grounds that he was not feeling well, he left Herst shortly afterwards, although they were to have spent the evening together, and set out in search of Olga. He was not able to find her until two hours later, for, taking advantage of her freedom, she had left the hotel—two hours which he spent champing at the bit and wondering how to set about putting her on her guard without appearing to be involved.

His fertile brain found an easy solution to this last point as soon as she appeared. Curtailing the usual endearments, for the situation demanded urgent measures, he exclaimed plaintively:

"You know, you're lucky you're not a man."

"Why?"

"Because the secret police, who see killers everywhere, are going to declare war on unaccompanied male travellers."

Thereupon he reported Herst's conversation, stressing the probable searches that would be taking place as from the following day. There was one point about this that had been bothering him ever since the tour started, and the henchman's statements made his apprehension unbearable: Verveuil's luggage no doubt contained the rifle with telescopic sights which he had planned to use on the wedding day and which he was surely keeping with him for a better opportunity. He could only hope that the silly fool had provided himself with papers to assure him a good cover, but a snap check might reveal the weapon.

He considered this danger from every angle, even envisaging the possibility of arranging for the rifle to be handed over to himself, wrapped up like an innocuous parcel. (He himself was provided, thanks to Herst, with papers which rendered him above suspicion.) It was not only the difficulty he would have in bringing off this operation, while maintaining the integrity of his own person and without revealing anything of his schemes, which made him abandon this idea. Here again his inventive brain might have found some means of getting Olga to entrust him with a piece of luggage too cumbersome for herself. No, if he gave up this idea, it was because he considered such collaboration on his part to be contrary to the principle of neutrality by which he wished to abide and which old Tournette used to sum up in one of his maxims: the photographer must be impartial.

And so he merely concluded, in the same facetious tone he had assumed since the start of their conversation:

"Here's my advice to any killer. If he wants to make a success of his undertaking, he must not stop for the night in the same town in which the President is staying."

It was not a stroke of genius. It was even rather obvious, a little too direct in spite of his jocular tone, but in a situation like this there was no room for circumlocutions.

Having told Olga this, he left it to her this time to find a suitable excuse for leaving him early, which she managed with her usual presence of mind. When he got back to his room he smiled as he heard the slight noise she made as she drew back one of the shutters in her own. Much later, after putting out the light but remaining on watch by the window, he heard another noise in the next room and spotted a piece of paper floating down into the street, doubtless a hastily scribbled note, which a passer-by furtively picked up before vanishing into the darkness.

Gaur had noticed the person in question was wearing

a beard, but he had no difficulty in recognising Verveuil's gait. He shrugged his shoulders irritably. How
typical of that nitwit to disguise himself in this cloak-
and-dagger manner! It was a sure way of attracting
attention to himself. What further eccentricities were
to be expected from him? Anyway, he was warned of
the danger, that was the main thing. It remained to be
seen whether he would be able to keep out of range of
his enemies. He, Martial Gaur, was conscious of having
done all he could to protect him.

3

THE RINGING OF THE TELEPHONE disturbed Martial and
Olga as they lay side by side on a rumpled bed. They
had arrived at Marseilles in the afternoon, Malarche
being due to spend several days in this town, from where
he would be able to tour the departments of the south-
west.

"I hope it's Herst," he muttered. "He hasn't shown
a sign of life for the last three days and he's the only
person who knows my address."

It was Herst all right. He sounded distraught and
asked Martial if he could see him that very morning.

"Come any time you like."

"I'll be round in half an hour. May I come up to
your room? What I have to tell you is confidential,
needless to say."

"Of course. Is it important? I mean important for
me."

"Selfish fellow! Yes, I think so. But I also have a
favour to ask you."

Martial felt his heart thump and glanced at Olga
who seemed not to be listening.

"I'll be waiting for you."

He replaced the receiver and turned to her.

"I'm terribly sorry, darling, but you'll have to leave. Herst will be here in a moment."

She leaped out of bed and snatched up her clothes.

"Herst? He probably has some good news for you."

"I hope so. He wants to speak to me confidentially."

She flung her things into her own room which communicated with Martial's, hastily tidied the bed, opened the window to dispel the whiff of her scent and made sure that no other trace of her presence remained. Having assured herself that everything was in order, she kissed him with fervour.

"I'm off. If you go out with him, knock on my door when you come in, no matter how late it is. I'll be so happy if this is the opportunity you've been waiting for."

"I will, I promise."

She disappeared and each of them bolted the intercommunicating door. When Herst arrived, Martial at once noticed his strained features and the dark circles under his eyes.

"What news?"

The henchman asked for a drink and refused to open his mouth until he had drained his glass.

"Well, it's quite simple. If this trip lasts another two weeks, I'm going to have a nervous breakdown."

"As bad as that? Yet I've only seen the President twice, from far off, and he seemed perfectly relaxed and at ease."

"Relaxed?" Herst bellowed. "You mean utterly thoughtless. He spends his time surrounded by the crowds. He slips between our fingers like an eel. It's not courage, I tell you, it's just foolhardiness; that's what it is. He doesn't even realise the risks he's running."

"Aren't you taking the job too much to heart? Aren't you exaggerating those risks? You've had no further cause for alarm, have you? The scaffolding business?"

"Nothing new in that direction. The investigation seems to be marking time."

"Good. After all, there were only vague suspicions on that score. In fact the trip seems to be proceeding without a single snag. He has had an enthusiastic reception everywhere, as far as I could see. The occasional boos from malcontents have been quickly drowned by the applause. It's my belief his enemies have realised the game is up for them and they've gone to ground, discouraged."

"That's what you think, is it?" Herst growled. "That's the official view, I know, carefully fostered, what's more, by his followers as well as by his opponents ... Well, let me tell you something, if you swear not to repeat it, because he doesn't want the incident to leak out. He feels it will detract from his increasing popularity. To cut a long story short, there has already been an attempt on his life."

"What!"

Martial Gaur felt the blood drain from his cheeks and was unable to suppress a gesture of fury.

"Exactly. It happened in Avignon. Oh, it was a badly organised job.... A sort of fanatic, a lunatic or semi-lunatic, who had no chance of bringing it off. We, the bodyguard, didn't even have to intervene. He was spotted by an inspector, with a loaded revolver bulging under his mackintosh. The incident passed unnoticed. All the same, he was less than ten yards from Malarche when he was arrested, just as he was reaching for his weapon."

"Do you know who he is?"

"A man by the name of Aralides, or something like that. A Greek anyway. But what does that matter to you?"

"To me? Oh, nothing," said Martial, making an effort to conceal the fright he had had.

"It seems the fellow's slightly off his head and was acting on his own initiative. All the same, it shows you I'm right to sleep with one eye open."

"But good heavens! . . ."

Martial Gaur now felt overwhelmed by a rage he could scarcely control and had to grip the arm of his chair to conceal the tremor of his hands. He suddenly had the feeling that shadowy legions of lunatics or fanatics were mounting a conspiracy against him and doing their utmost to frustrate his own plans.

"Good heavens! What the devil are your security services doing? Dangerous madmen can't be allowed to stroll about in the street during a presidential visit!"

Herst appeared to consider this remark and the tone in which it was uttered as a personal slight and felt the need to justify himself.

"Don't worry. We do keep an eye on them. Only every loonie isn't labelled. After all, we're not as slip-shod as you seem to think, since this one was spotted in time."

"In time? Only just. Is that good enough? Only ten yards from the President, you said!"

Gaur was unable to calm down despite his efforts and, in his blind indignation, sounded as though he was accusing the bodyguards of inefficiency. The President's security was now causing more anxiety to him than to the luckless Herst.

"And he himself makes our task all the more difficult," the latter protested in a crestfallen tone. "He keeps making last-minute changes in the established plans, completely invalidating our precautions. And that silly little wife of his is even worse. . . . Didn't she drag him out into the street the other day, at nine in the morning, whereas his appearance was planned for ten o'clock? . . . An escapade, that's all it was. Both of them by themselves, unguarded, arm in arm like a couple of lovers, merely wearing dark glasses as disguise. . . . Childish behaviour! Utterly childish!"

"Childish! Is that all you have to say? I call it sheer madness," Martial Gaur exclaimed, carried away once more by his indignation. "And you, who should be sticking to him like a leech all the time, go and let him commit such follies! Besides, you swore you would tell me if there was an opportunity. . . ."

"I didn't know about it myself, I tell you. He didn't warn anyone. It's a fancy that seems suddenly to have occurred to his wife's bird-like mind, and he allowed himself to be dragged off like a little boy. . . . They spent a quarter of an hour outside, strolling about, window-shopping, pretending to be foreign tourists. Just imagine! Luckily no one recognised them. The greatest follies sometimes come off. It was his valet who notified me. . . . I can tell you, when he came back, President or no President, I requested a private interview with him in no uncertain terms. He granted it. He looked rather sheepish. At that point, protocol or no protocol, I almost lost my temper. . . ."

"No wonder," the photographer growled. "In your place I should have threatened to hand in my resignation."

"That's more or less what I did. I wish you could have been there. He realised he had gone too far. I assure you he looked like a schoolboy caught red-handed playing truant. Only the thing is, I can't be angry with him for long. I'm fond of him and I try to put myself in his place. . . . Anyway he promised not to do it again, at least without warning me in advance."

"That's the least he could do," Gaur muttered in a calmer but still rather dry tone.

"Because he intends to do it again, and quite soon too. That's what I want to talk to you about, because I don't forget my promises, whatever you say. This time it will be a real escapade which will last the whole day. So, since he can't manage it on his own, he not only notifies Uncle Herst but actually makes him responsible for organising it. Do you realise the job he's asking me to do? On the whole I'm not sure I don't prefer it this way. It's worse for me if something happens, but that can't be helped. Well anyway, I've been given the delicate mission of planning a day's outing for him on the seaside, in some quiet spot where the two of them can bill and coo in peace with no bodyguards around them—they don't want to see us, hear us or feel us breathing down their necks. It seems we're not very popular with her."

"Thanks for letting me know," said Martial, who

had completely recovered his composure and was glancing furtively at the communicating door between the two rooms. "When is it going to happen, and where?"

"As to when, I can tell you straight away. Next Wednesday. It's the only time he has free. He's meant to be having a day off then in a country house in the hills, but in fact he won't arrive there till the evening. . . ."

"Good," said Martial Gaur with relief. "That leaves me five days to get things ready."

"As to where, I don't know yet, and this is where I want to ask you a favour."

"What can I do for you?" the photographer asked with a trace of excitement, for he was beginning to realise what his friend was after and had a glimpse of fresh prospects fraught with possibilities for himself.

"This is the situation. The President's a good fellow, but I haven't time to deal with this particular problem. I can't keep an eye on him and also reconnoitre the beaches. Nor can I ask the other policemen to help me. They certainly wouldn't agree in any case and the secret would be out at once. So I thought of you. . . ."

"Of me?" Martial stammered in a sort of ecstasy. "Of me?"

"Yes. After all, you're interested in this business. You haven't anything else to do and I know I can count on your discretion. Can you do me the favour of prospecting along the coast and finding somewhere that will satisfy everyone, not only the young couple who want a pleasant spot, not only myself who am concerned with security, but also you, since you're in the know, so that you can take the photo you've always

129

dreamed of? The more I think of it, the more I'm convinced that this job is right up your street. What do you say?"

"I accept," said Martial, doing his utmost to conceal his enthusiam. "I accept gladly, because you don't know how rare and valuable it is for a photographer to be able to choose the setting for himself."

4

AND SO MARTIAL GAUR set out on the following day in search of a beach which would satisfy a variety of requirements. He had of course asked Olga to come with him. Her opinion was invaluable in this delicate mission.

She had not needed much persuasion, and the gaiety she displayed this morning, as she sat by his side, was anything but feigned. She could not but thank the powers that be for Herst's unhoped-for suggestion. Since Martial likewise regarded the henchman's idea as a heaven-sent inspiration, it was in an atmosphere of exultation that they drove off together along the coast.

The evening before, he had not taken long to inform her of these latest developments. When he got back to his hotel, after seeing Herst home, she was in bed but not asleep.

"You realise, I'm going to choose the setting myself! It will be a sensational picture, Olga. Just think. . . . All the trump cards. The subject: a Head of State, alone with the woman he loves on a deserted beach, and the surroundings . . . What I want is a gorgeous

131

landscape," he exclaimed in a fit of romantic enthusiasm, " . . . a cove. That's it, I can already see it: a cove carved out of the rocks, with a background of pine-clad cliffs; and bathed in light, above all light, a light accentuating the splendours of the Mediterranean and Provence."

"You're right," she murmured in a slightly husky voice, veiled by the excitement her lover had just communicated to her. "A sumptuous setting, worthy of the scene. I can also see the cove. It exists. We'll discover it."

He had sat down on the edge of her bed and, in a transport of emotion, leant forward, his muscles flexed, pressing down with his clenched fists on either side of his mistress's body. He was enthralled to be so perfectly understood and to discern in her dilated pupils an elation equal to his own. At that moment there was no murky ulterior motive in his mind and they went on talking for a long time in a sort of ecstasy.

He was driving his own car, specially adapted for his leg, forcing himself to keep the speed down, in the state of mind of a pedigree bloodhound on the scent of a noble quarry. They had driven past the Marseilles beach and those of the near-by villages without so much as glancing at them. The sand here was anything but inviting and, though the season had barely started, there were already a fair amount of bathers.

"Too many people and far too commonplace. A picture-postcard setting," he had declared. "Not at all the sort of place that would appeal to Malarche who wants privacy and beauty."

She had agreed without a moment's hesitation.

"And I don't see anywhere you could hide to take a photo," she added with a touch of anxiety.

He looked at her tenderly and, though still at the wheel, could not resist giving her a furtive kiss.

"We agree about everything, you and I, darling. It's out of the question."

But the landscape presently changed and the coast soon revealed its marvels when they turned off down the new Route des Calanques, which had been completed only a couple of months before, after endless confabulations and hindrances from the owners of the seaside bungalows who feared their tranquillity would be jeopardised by throwing open to motorised tourists a thoroughfare that had hitherto been used only by the hardier kind of pedestrian tripper. The road skirted the coast in countless meanders, forcing its way through pine-clad cliffs of white rock punctuated here and there by little creeks.

They stopped several times to inspect some of these havens, without being able to find a single one that satisfied their thirst for perfection. They finally came to a halt above a fairly large cove. Here, struck by the beauty of the site, they exchanged a long glance, then turned off down a side road leading to it and got out of the car to examine it at close quarters, for some of its natural advantages were immediately obvious. A few fishermen's houses occupied the inside of the bay, overlooking a makeshift harbour where two or three boats and a pleasure launch lay at anchor. There was a rough path hewn out of the granite leading away from the hamlet, in which not a soul was visible, down to a creek where the clear water, lapping a semi-circle of white sand, could not fail to entice anyone who liked sea-bathing. They sat down on a rock and both embarked on a meticulous analysis of the setting.

"It's not too bad," Olga finally said, with an interrogatory glance at him.

"Not bad at all," he echoed under his breath.

It would certainly have been difficult not to be moved by the beauty of the landscape. He fancied he detected a faint reservation in Olga's tone, however, and he respected her judgement. He himself was unable to make up his mind.

He sat in silence beside her for some time, assailed by a feeling of uneasiness which he could not fathom. All round him he seemed to see, and to feel in the very depths of his being, a profusion of factors favourable to the birth of a masterpiece. He longed to get down to work but was tormented by the thought that he might be labouring under a delusion. He was afraid of deciding definitely on this spot when there might be a better one and thereby committing himself irretrievably. For several interminable minutes he endured all the suffering, all the torments of the creative artist.

Certain precepts which old Tournette had dinned into him in the course of his apprenticeship kept buzzing through his brain. "The photographer must be capable of creating in advance, in his mind's eye, a complete image of the ultimate exposure" . . . . "Never forget that every detail will be automatically reproduced and that some details, which the human eye does not perceive in nature, may look monstrous in a photograph and disfigure it irreparably. . . ."

134

Above all he had to visualise the main subject in relation to the setting. He therefore concentrated exclusively on this subject for some time, abiding by his personal rule which was, despite Tournette's advice, to give it precedence over the details. He managed without much effort to conjure up the couple of lovers, Malarche and his young wife, lying side by side on the sand, relaxed, inhaling the fresh air, intent on making the most of their few hours' freedom.

It was at this moment, taking advantage of their immobility, that Verveuil would adjust his sights. Where would the killer position himself? Without doubt beyond that row of pine trees among the rocks, where he could find a suitable hide-out, but no closer. The range was slightly less than a hundred yards, and this fact gave rise to the same doubt he had felt when inspecting the house with the scaffolding. Verveuil claimed to be sure of himself at this distance, but his intolerable vanity debarred him from being trusted implicitly. Gaur had the feeling that Olga was extremely worried by this question and she was bound to know her accomplice and his capabilities even better than he did. His eyes met hers and he detected in them an unvoiced anxiety, the same uncertainty he had noticed in her tone of voice when she said, "Not too bad." However, he could not very well ask her opinion straight out, as he would have liked to do. This was contrary to the rules of the game.

He muttered again between clenched teeth, "Yes, it's not too bad," as though he was trying to convince himself. After all, at less than a hundred yards, there was surely every chance of success. He dismissed this aspect of the subject from his mind and embarked on other considerations. He had devoted sufficient attention to the problems of the others. He certainly could not be accused of selfishness. It was time to think of his own observation post, the post of the photographer.

This he was able to choose for himself to a certain extent. It was agreed with Herst that he should not attempt to conceal himself among the rocks (it was difficult for him with his game leg to behave like a mountain goat. He would take up his position in advance, in a tent, masquerading as one of those campers who are to be encountered everywhere along this coast, even in the most inaccessible spots. He would pretend to be asleep and would be able to operate at his ease under cover, without being seen. He examined the ground carefully. He would pitch his tent above the beach, overlooking the whole stage. It was a satisfactory arrangement, at first sight. And yet . . .

He felt a sharp twinge of vexation and wrinkled his brow. On closer examination it seemed to him that the only really suitable spot from which to get an overall view was where they happened to be standing at that moment. But, because of the shape of the creek and the almost inevitable location of the couple, he would have a deplorable background: a barrier of bare rocks, dazzling white, which would make his exposure blurred, even with the best colour filters. No sight of the sea, not even a ripple. His photograph would look as though it had been taken against a blank wall. It was out of the question.

He sighed and scanned the horizon again in search of another position. The lie of the land was not very helpful. He might perhaps move over to the left, slightly higher up among the rocks. Yes, from there he would just be able to get a view of the couple with a stretch of sea behind them and a small section of cliff: a passable but far from perfect background. Besides . . .

Besides . . . He grimaced with disappointment and gave vent to an angry oath, while Olga looked at him in surprise. Was he out of his mind not to have thought of this straight away? It was absolutely obvious. With his game leg, he would never have time, after taking his first exposure, to scramble down from this position among the rocks and rush across to the beach to take a close-up of the victim at point-blank range. This document, which was to be the king-pin of the series and which he could not renounce at any price, would elude him from here. It would take him several minutes to cover that distance over such uneven ground. Herst and his acolytes, who would surely not be far off, would arrive before him.

"Let's go and have a look elsewhere," he said abruptly to Olga. "I'm sure we can find something better."

He was glad to detect approval in the sigh of relief she heaved.

He had almost allowed himself to be captivated and led astray by the beauty of the surroundings. It had been a close thing. He congratulated himself on his lucky escape, concluding that no one is ever difficult enough towards himself and that the creative artist, in his search for perfection, must sometimes be able to moderate his inspiration in favour of a punctilious and inflexible critical faculty.

AT A GESTURE FROM OLGA who was riding pillion behind him, Verveuil stopped his motor-cycle on a bend overlooking the creek shortly after branching off down a stony road which led towards it.

"There it is."

Without leaving his machine, like a tourist in a hurry, Verveuil hastily scanned the horizon. Unlike Gaur, he was indifferent to the beauty of the landscape and viewed the surroundings from a purely utilitarian point of view.

"I think Gaur was absolutely inspired," Olga went on. "I did my utmost to induce his decision. From here, all the trump cards are in our hand."

Verveuil pursed his lips and did not reply directly. Instinctively aware of his accomplice's superiority, though refusing to admit it, he had confidence in her judgement but did not wish to agree with her too quickly. He made a show of taking stock of objections which would never occur to a subordinate.

"Let's have a closer look," he said with a self-important air. "You're quite sure Herst has agreed to this choice?"

"Martial brought him here this very morning to show him his discovery and he said he was satisfied. He raised no objection. This is where Pierre Malarche will be coming the day after tomorrow."

After having indeed explored a considerable number of sites and having almost decided, for want of anything better, on one of them which offered some of the required advantages, Gaur had finally come upon this marvellous stretch of coast which satisfied all of them.

It was an exceptionally lovely creek, carved out of cliffs which erosion had sculpted into fantastic contours that made the photographer's heart beat faster. Lack of fresh water had so far preserved it from holiday huts and bungalows. Only on Sundays people from Marseilles occasionally came and had a picnic here, and a few trippers camped here during the holidays. Extremely few: tourists preferred less isolated spots. It could be reached by car along a rough track or, at a pinch, on foot along an old path now more or less obliterated by landslides and vegetation.

It was this path which the two accomplices were looking for, taking care not to be observed. They found it presently and followed it. Verveuil studied the ground minutely and stopped from time to time to take his bearings. He growled at certain bad patches where the **brambles hampered him** and carefully tugged them aside. He was obviously thinking of his line of withdrawal.

They eventually reached the last thicket, which was as close to the creek as they could have wished. The sandy beach was less than fifty yards away. Verveuil gave a nod of approval. After a short reconnaissance

139

he chose a position under a pine-tree sprouting between two blocks of granite, where the undergrowth concealed him completely. He picked up a stick and went through the motions of aiming at a point on the beach.

"No matter what spot he chooses, the field of fire is good," he said. "I'm beginning to think you're right. We've never been so close to our goal. . . . Let's hope they don't take other security measures which we can't foresee."

"I tell you there won't be any others. Herst has explained it all to Gaur, deploring this lack of caution. But Malarche's orders are categorical. The three usual henchmen will be here, that's all. Even then they will have to keep out of sight of the couple. They'll be on the side road more than three hundred yards away. The President has insisted on this."

"How can you be so sure?"

"Herst has taken Martial into his confidence over this business and you know there are no secrets between the latter and me," she said, shrugging her shoulders. "I've been told all the details. After a great deal of hesitation, Herst has even decided not to have the roads guarded by the local police. From the moment he realised it was impossible to maintain a total surveillance, he considered that the best security was absolute secrecy."

"Except towards his friend Gaur," Verveuil chuckled.

"Except towards Gaur, who's above suspicion and whose discretion he cannot question. . . . So once Malarche has been dealt with, since you're quite sure of yourself, by the time the three bodyguards have reached the beach, come to the rescue of their boss and discovered from where the shot came, we'll be well away."

"Yes," Verveuil repeated. "It looks as if it's in the bag. In two days' time the country will be rid of that impostor and at last we'll have a decent Government."

This sort of ranting left Olga completely indifferent. Her gaze was fixed on a point on the beach. She stood there for some time, her face tensed, her teeth clenched, as though oblivious of her companion. She finally roused herself from her reverie and spoke as though to herself.

"I wonder if Martial will ever know how helpful he has been to us and what role I have played in relation to him."

"Do you care?"

She did not bother to reply and pursued her own thoughts.

"I think he will. He'll realise when he notices my disappearance."

"Herst will suspect him of careless talk, since he's the only one in the secret," Verveuil muttered in sudden alarm. "And from one thing to another . . ."

"Don't worry. I'll disappear without trace. All the addresses I've given him are false."

"I hope you didn't disclose your real identity to him."

"Don't worry about that, I tell you," she remarked disdainfully.

These details were of no importance to her once the end had been attained. It was with a touch of condescension that she endeavoured again to reassure her accomplice.

141

"In any case Martial won't mention me. I'm certain of that."

"It would indeed be tantamount to admitting his indiscretion," he agreed after a moment's reflection.

It was obvious she had no wish to say anything further on this matter. Verveuil shrugged his shoulders.

"After all, you must know him better than I do by this time."

"With him, there was only one thing I was afraid of," she went on as pensively as ever, as though pursuing a monologue.

She had feared that Gaur might ask her to come with him and be there when he took the photograph. It would then have been impossible for her to elude the subsequent police enquiries. But no, he had been perfect, as usual.

"He actually brought this question up himself, but in order to reassure me. It had occurred to him that I might like to be with him. He understood only too well, he said, how much such a spectacle was bound to arouse my curiosity. With great consideration—he has always been extremely considerate towards me—he asked me if I wouldn't be too disappointed not to be in on the party. It would have handicapped him. He likes to operate on his own for important assignments and he looks upon this one as the crowning point of his career. So I'm free—once again, thanks to him."

"He won't be disappointed about the photograph," Verveuil sniggered. "On the whole we'll be doing that fool a favour in return, in our own fashion."

Olga shrugged her shoulders and made no reply. There was nothing else for them to see. They retraced their steps and got back to the road. Here they made sure there was enough cover to conceal the motor-cycle completely in the undergrowth, for it was the same vehicle they were going to use on the day after tomorrow. The dismantled rifle would be carried in a fishing-rod case. A couple on a motor-cycle, with this gear, was not likely to attract attention on the coast. Every detail of the operation seemed to be settled.

Before leaving, Verveuil made a final allusion to Martial Gaur.

"I quite agree with you," he said, with another snigger. "That idiot Gaur is perfect for us. He's smoothed out all our difficulties and solved almost all our problems, and is blissfully unconcious of the fact. Like you, I'm now pretty sure he'll never suspect the role we've made him play. He's really too gullible for words."

143

6

ON TUESDAY, the eve of the great day, Martial Gaur came and took up his position in the creek. He was feeling brisk and alert, elated by the sense of excitement known only to adventurous men of action just before they embark on the final hazardous stage of an audacious undertaking, at the end of which their feverish eyes discern the magical glimmer of success.

It had been a long time since he had known such periods of keen suspense, the most thrilling periods in his life, and the unhoped-for delight of feeling anew the enthusiasm of his youth added to his exultation. This was the main reason for his moving to the creek before the curtain went up. He wanted to spend this armed vigil on the spot, to make his final material preparations, granted, but above all to collect his thoughts. Every work of art demands intense preliminary concentration and solitude.

But his other reason for coming so early was to facilitate the conspirators' plan. With him out of the way, Olga would have complete freedom to pack her bags, leave their hotel in Marseilles and join her accom-

144

plice, who must surely be needing her. Maybe she would leave a message for him, giving some excuse for her hasty departure and informing him of her painful decision to disappear from his life for ever? Every now and then he found himself imagining the wording of this message and he could not help smiling.

He parked his car some distance from the creek without attempting to conceal it. The presence of a vehicle was normal near a tourist's tent and would cause no offence to the President. The creek was not completely deserted this afternoon. Three young men, who had no doubt come from a neighbouring beach, were bathing off a boat. They paid no attention to Martial and their presence did not bother him in any way.

He unpacked his camping equipment and started pitching his tent on the spot he had chosen after countless technical considerations through which he had sifted minutely with all the resources of his experience. This required little effort in spite of the handicap of his leg. He found his gestures were as nimble and accurate as in the good old days. He had already used this gear on several occasions as a hiding-place, and the direction in which he had to site it so as to operate in the best conditions had been settled in his head for several days.

When he had finished he smiled with pleasure as he looked at his canvas shelter. Then he went back to his car, unloaded the precious tools of his trade and arranged them methodically in one corner of the tent. The cameras, the rolls of film, the colour filters and light meters, all had already been subjected to a meticulous selection and scrutiny. There was nothing more to do but wait.

145

The sun had disappeared behind the tall cliffs surrounding the creek. The three young men had boarded their boat and were moving off. He was alone in the creek, which still retained the heat of the day. He set up a deck-chair and placed a glass within arm's reach.

Everything seemed to be in perfect working order. All that remained was to reap the reward of his crafty preparations. The setting was perfect. There was no point in inspecting it again this evening; he would have plenty of time in the morning and the light would then be better. It remained to be seen if all the actors were conversant with their roles. It seemed to him that they were, but he still nurtured a few anxieties on this score. And so, as he sat down facing the darkening sea to make a final mental inspection of the most intricate cogs in the machine, he thought straight away of Verveuil and his accomplice, trying to imagine their state of mind and to visualise their movements in the course of this evening.

It was a game in which he had indulged for a long time. He knew that Verveuil was staying not in Marseilles (he had made a point of putting him on his guard against such a rash move) but in the outskirts. The place in which he would attract least attention at this time of the year, and where he would also be within striking distance, was some bathing resort, maybe Cassis or La Ciotat. He saw them both this evening sitting, like himself, in front of the sea, probably on the terrace of an hotel, Verveuil still sporting his false beard perhaps, feeling slightly nervous on the whole, making an effort to maintain the composure of a hero, trying more than ever to convince himself that he was the man of destiny.

In this month of June the terrace would be deserted, or almost. They would have chosen a corner in which they could not be overheard. From time to time one of them would make a remark or ask a question in an undertone. Olga, equally on tenterhooks, would be anxious to know if her acolyte had thought of everything.

"You're sure we're not at the mercy of some stupid accident—a breakdown, for instance?"

Verveuil would reply that he was not a child and had left nothing to chance. There were new tyres on his motor-cycle and the engine had been checked a few days before.

"What about the rifle? Is it safely hidden away? There's no chance of missing, is there? You're sure of your aim?"

"My dear girl," Verveuil would reply in a protective tone. "The gun is dismantled, safely concealed in a padlocked box, and I tried it out only last week. The ammunition is top quality. As I've told you before, just leave it to me."

Thus did Martial Gaur try to appease his own anxiety, by imagining reassuring replies. The weapon in particular continued to give him a great deal of worry. He would have liked to be certain that it was perfectly adapted for the operation and felt disturbed, he who was manipulating the strings of the intrigue, at being more or less completely ignorant on this subject, condemned to fruitless speculations.

As for Olga, he once again asked himself the question which had been bothering him for some time.

Would Olga be accompanying the killer? Would she be by his side at the moment he fired? Or would she stay behind on the road by the vehicle? Or indeed, now that her role was over, had she already left the district? This was not particularly important, but he felt annoyed and almost guilty to be still in ignorance of certain details of the scenario. He hesitated for some time, as though confronted by some irritating problem, subjected all the data in his possession to a minute analysis, and finally convinced himself that she would be on the spot beside her accomplice. She would want to savour the spectacle of her revenge. Besides, she probably did not have boundless confidence in Verveuil's resolution in the event of a mishap. This rational conclusion that Olga would be present gave him a certain degree of relief, without his being able to explain exactly why.

There remained his own role. He knew it by heart. He would have all the time he needed to run through it in his head for the last time in the morning, in daylight, while he was making a final inspection of the setting.

He spent a somewhat restless night in his sleeping-bag but nevertheless managed to doze off for a few hours. He was wakened at dawn by the sound of an engine and listened intently. It was a motor-cycle. The noise, reverberating from the cliffs in the early morning silence, stopped all of a sudden. Martial felt an intense intellectual satisfaction, which blossomed into a smile. He was certainly going through a period of outstanding perspicacity. Endeavouring, the evening before, to put himself in the conspirators' shoes, he had thought that a motor-cycle was the most suitable vehicle to conceal for an occasion of this sort, and the handiest for making a quick get-away.

He got up and sat by the window of his tent, pricking up his ears. There was not a breath of air and the creek was barely stirred by a few soundless puffs. At the end of a quarter of an hour or so he fancied he heard a sound of crackling in the thickets between him and the main road. He was not mistaken. Someone was moving through the undergrowth. Verveuil, beyond all doubt. Olga was with him—of this he now felt certain. They were taking the path, as he had likewise foreseen. It was the safest route for them.

They were getting into position well in advance. Just as well. Freed from his worry on this score, he could not help severely criticising their approach which was anything but discreet: he could follow their progress by ear. Not only by ear but also ... Yes, his eyes had not deceived him: a bush over there had quivered, then another slightly lower down. Any camper who happened to be here would have noticed their arrival. Martial Gaur, who naturally held Verveuil responsible for this lack of caution, gave an angry shrug and muttered:

"How much longer is he going to go on drawing attention to himself like this? A good thing he arrived early!"

Another bush was shaken as though by a gust of wind, one of the last bits of cover before the beach.

"I do hope he stops. If he comes down any further he'll be in full view."

But the bush quivered several times, then the undergrowth resumed its silent immobility. Gaur calmed down and even smiled again: the killer was taking up his position in the very place he himself had determined.

Verveuil, who had wheeled his motor-cycle into a dense thicket a little way off the road, carefully obliterated his tracks. Then he picked up a case which seemed to be rather heavy, slung it over his shoulder and, followed by Olga, set off through the pine-trees along the path. She was wearing shorts and a blouse; he the sort of khaki suit favoured by weekend anglers. There was nothing to distinguish them from a couple of townsfolk preparing for a day's outing by the sea. She had even provided herself with a picnic basket, from which the neck of a reassuring bottle protruded.

He swore under his breath as he arrived near the creek. In spite of their precautions, in spite of the sandals they were wearing, it was impossible to prevent the crackling of the bone-dry undergrowth.

"He's liable to hear us. Let's hope he doesn't take it into his head to come and have a stroll round here."

An encounter with Gaur was evidently what he most feared. He was the only person to whom they would be unable to account for their presence.

"I'd be surprised if he did. At this moment, if he's awake, he's thinking of one thing only—his photo. Furthermore, it's difficult for him to move about on ground like this."

They reached the chosen position. Verveuil put his load down on the ground, picked up the stick he had left in the fork of the pine-tree and made a final check.

"Perfect," he said under his breath.

"Can I have a look?"

He shifted slightly to make room for her between the two rocks. Like him, she went through the motions of taking aim, with the stick pressed against her shoulder and held between her fingers. With a slow traversing movement, she swept the whole beach, lingering for a moment on a certain point where she already saw in her mind's eye a body lying on the sand. This body seemed an unmissable target, even for someone like herself who was not trained to handle firearms.

"We've got him," she whispered. "Are you going to assemble the rifle?"

He was against this. They still had several hours to wait and, well concealed though they were, it was just possible that a tripper might come across them. It would then be easy for them to pretend to be a couple of lovers loitering in the wood.

"I'll assemble it just before Malarche arrives. About eleven o'clock you said, didn't you?"

"He'll be leaving Marseilles on the dot of eleven, I'm sure of that. Herst has been obliged to draw up a detailed timetable, to enable him to leave his residence without being noticed. He can be here twenty minutes later."

"I'll assemble the rifle at eleven. At that hour Gaur won't budge from his tent even if he hears a slight noise."

On their side too, everything seemed to be in perfect working order. They settled down to a long wait, taking it in turns to keep watch on the rough track leading down to the creek.

151

7

THE PHOTOGRAPHER, on the other hand, had no reason to remain in hiding. The conspirators were aware of his presence. He opened his tent and stood outside facing the location he had had such difficulty in finding and which today he regarded almost as his own creation. In front of him the sea, the rocks and the pines formed an ideal setting, the very setting of which he had dreamed for his exploit, a setting which was finally assuming its significance in the early-morning light.

The sun was beginning to rise above the cliffs. The blocks of granite assumed more clearly defined contours. The water in the creek turned green. The shingle started shimmering and the grey sand was tinged with white and ochre. The photographer picked up his camera, lifted the view-finder to his eye with the gesture of a hunter on the look-out, and slowly swept the beach.

It was ten o'clock. He again checked the strength of the light and analysed its quality with the help of various instruments. He had carried out this operation more than a dozen times since dawn. All was well. The light would be perfect in an hour or so. He put the camera back in its case next to another slightly different one reserved for the close-up. Then he sat down at the entrance to his tent to immerse himself once again in every aspect of the setting and embark on a dress rehearsal in his mind.

First of all he looked up at the sky and felt overwhelmed with gratitude to the gods of Provence for endowing this earth with a firmament of such serenity. Not a cloud in sight. The sheet of uninterrupted blue showed not the slightest gap. Having spent the preceding days studying the weather reports, tortured by the thought that a storm might cloud the atmosphere, he inwardly uttered a heartfelt act of grace. There was no accident of this sort to be feared.

He lowered his gaze to the horizon, without his eye being able to find the slightest grounds for criticism. Sky and sea formed a general composition of perfect harmony, so well attuned that it was impossible to tell which engendered the magic of the other. The photographer felt so elated at the sight of this luminous miracle that tears came into his eyes.

He forced himself to recover his composure and slowly, taking infinite care not to overlook a single detail, switched his gaze still lower to the creek, lingering on the cliffs which framed the majestic inflow of the sea. Thereupon, in spite of his determination to keep a clear head and observe the landscape today only with a severely critical eye, he was once again unable to withstand a romantic emotion closely akin to ecstasy. These cliffs of white rock, carved out in tall needles whose tortured contours seemed to have been placed here with supreme artistry to interrupt the uniformity of the background at exactly the required spot, looked like columns marking the threshold of a prodigious temple sculpted by nature for the accomplishment of sacred mysteries.

From here, starting from the dazzling bare granite of the peaks, continuing along the first sparse row of rust-coloured pine-trees, then the denser forest, and ending up with the gleaming pebbles on the water's edge, he discovered a range of outstanding hues, a symphony whose general appearance and individual detail he was able to grasp simultaneously from where he was standing. . . . Yes, the setting was perfect, without a single lapse of taste, worthy in every respect of the scene which was going to be enacted in an hour or two's time, this scene which the moment had come to evoke for the last time.

The transition from the setting to the main subject was afforded by an examination of the undergrowth fringing the beach on his left. His gaze rested on a particular pine-tree between two rocky outcrops. From there the shot would come, a sort of signal for his own appearance on stage. It was not beyond the bounds of possibility, in fact it was even more than likely, that at the last moment the marksman would tend to lean forward as he poked the barrel of his weapon through the branches, and even reveal part of his face. Just for an instant, no doubt: this was one of those details which the human eye, attracted by a profusion of images, is unable to grasp but which the faithful camera never fails to register. His position had been so well chosen that this detail would certainly be caught by the lens focused on the general scene, even though it was at the limit of its field of view.

154

But only on one condition: only if Pierre Malarche placed himself exactly at the desired spot. If he didn't, the killer's face and weapon would escape notice. After all, this was not essential.... Maybe not, but another consideration lent the President's position such importance for the photographer that he bitterly bemoaned the fact that the role of this particular actor was more or less completely out of his control, so much so indeed that he had omitted to include it in the mental rehearsal he had carried out the evening before.

In point of fact the spot where the President chose to lie down was of considerable importance. Martial Gaur's gaze now rested on a specific area, which afforded the conditions of total success. This narrow strip of ground fulfilled a desperate hope, a desire more violent than all the other emotions which had nagged at him in the course of the last few weeks. If Malarche placed himself here, his picture would be a masterpiece. It would be less successful if the President chose to lie down a few yards further on, in which case it would fail to take complete advantage of all the resources, all the splendours of this miraculous setting which sky, sea and earth had combined to create in the course of centuries for an artist to exploit in the fraction of a second.

This was how Martial Gaur's exceptionally shrewd mind considered the problem at least. Why? Because at this precise spot, a particular detail—only a detail, to be sure, but an odd detail, one of those details that transfigure a work of art—would lend his picture that additional touch of fantasy which genuine artists pursue all their life, which indoor photographers endeavour to evoke artificially by a quaint combination of incongruous objects, but which nature hardly ever grants to the press photographer. Straight in line with this precise spot, but much further off, on the left side of the creek, a group of three bare rocks, slightly darker in hue than the rest, stood out in sharp relief against the background; and the shape of these rocks suggested some huge bird of prey, with wings outspread but head and neck hanging limp, as though mortally wounded. In the general view, taken from his tent, the eagle appeared to be hovering above the main subject, and the photographer's eye had instantly grasped the striking impression which a detail like this was bound to make on a public attracted by romantic symbolism. Even the purest artist sometimes has to think of his public. Tournette himself considered that a perfect picture ought to appeal to aesthetes, magazine editors and shopgirls alike.

The image of the eagle had forcibly obtruded on Martial Gaur's mind ever since his first visit to the creek with Olga. To induce the President to lie down here and nowhere else, he had momentarily interrupted his meditation the evening before and strolled along this narrow strip of sand. He had carefully cleared it of every twig and scrap of driftwood that might have put off a potential bather. He would have sifted the sand with his own fingers to make it finer if he had had the time. This morning he thought it looked irresistible. Malarche could not, must not, fail to notice it.

If he did, however (Gaur had to be prepared for every contingency), if he stationed himself with his wife a little further on, the first picture would not be perfect. The wounded bird would not lie directly above the main subject but slightly to the right or to the left. In this case he might perhaps be able to recoup on the close-up he intended to take.

This close-up, the very conception of which sometimes made him tremble himself during his finest hours of hope and which was to create an even more intense sensation than the preceding pictures, brought him back to the consideration of his own role and the most delicate part of his task. He had started rehearsing his movements ever since his discovery of the creek. His first exposure and the rifle shot would be simultaneous. He would straight away take another snap, from the same place; he was trained to carry out this sort of operation in less than a second. Then he would seize the other camera and make his way as fast as possible towards the body lying on the sand, photograph it at point-blank range and perhaps catch its final convulsions. He would certainly have enough time for this in spite of the handicap of his leg. The distance he had to cover was not enormous, and the ground not too uneven. The evening before, he had timed himself over this course, carefully noting the obstacles which might make him stumble. He could reach the victim in a few seconds. Then, by lying flat on the ground, he might be able to position himself in line with the three rocks. Herein lay his second chance.

But the success of this unique document still depended on a number of circumstances which it was difficult to foresee with any degree of accuracy. First and foremost, the position of the victim. This was likewise independent of his own will. Would his face be turned upwards, which would facilitate the operation? Would it be in profile? Looking towards the sea or at the ground? The shrewdest mind in the world could not determine these factors in advance. They depended not only on Pierre Malarche's behaviour but also on chance, imponderables and . . .

Heavens above! There was really no reason for being so pleased with himself the evening before and congratulating himself on having determined the movements of his characters so meticulously. With only one hour to go before the curtain rose, he now realised there were dreadful loopholes in his arrangements. He had not given a single thought to one of the main characters, who would certainly have a part to play, and a part that might prove important—the President's wife. He had implicitly regarded her up to now as a minor figure on the stage. He strove to repair this neglect, but here again it was difficult.

Who could predict the reactions of a young woman who would probably have lost her head? Martial had seen her only once or twice at a distance. He had examined photographs of her out of professional curiosity. He remembered her having a slender figure and an attractive, almost childish face with regular features, nothing in fact to distinguish her from the girls who were his usual clients. Who could imagine her probably senseless reactions when she saw the man she loved bleeding to death practically in her arms? Would she rush off in panic, shouting for help? Would she, on the contrary, fling herself on her husband's body and cling to it in despair? After all, maybe this would give an additional poignancy to the scene which would appeal to a great many people. Personally, Martial Gaur did not think so. The artist must not seek an *accumulation of effects* but aim, on the contrary, at cohesion in emotion. To achieve this cohesion, he felt that attention should be focused on the main subject. Provided, of course, her untimely demonstrations did not completely mask this leading character who had to be kept continually in mind.

He shrugged his shoulders, deeming it superflous to indulge any further in fruitless speculations. He would act according to the circumstances. He would have to trust his eye and his reflexes. After drawing up his plans with the utmost care, the artist must be capable of modifying them instantly in the event of a mishap and, if necessary, revising them completely. This was another maxim he had learnt from old Tournette, on whose lessons and examples he had pondered deeply these last few days. Everything that could be catered for and organised had been dealt with. The rest was a matter of inspiration.

He consulted his watch impatiently, while a fresh anxiety assailed him: the thought that something might make the Head of State cancel his outing at the last moment. He was quickly reassured. Only a few minutes went by before the noise of an approaching motor made him sit up with a start.

After slowing down, the vehicle turned off down the rough track leading to the creek. It stopped some distance away. An almost voluptuous shiver went up Martial's spine when, a moment or two later, he saw the presidential couple appear round the last bend and make their way slowly down towards the sea.

8

WITH HIS ELBOWS RESTING ON THE CAR, a popular model specially hired for the occasion, Herst bleakly watched the couple as they sauntered off. He felt uneasy as he realised they would presently be out of sight round a bend in the road.

Before leaving him, the President had once again repeated his orders. Herst and his men were to approach no further, and Malarche also added in a rather disagreeable tone of voice that he had no wish to see anyone's head protruding from the bushes and spying on them, as had sometimes happened in similar circumstances. Since these instructions had been decreed by the President's wife, Herst knew that he not only risked losing his job if he disobeyed them but that he would also be the cause of a painful domestic scene and would incur the displeasure of a boss for whom he felt a deep attachment.

The two figures had reached the bend. Pierre Malarche turned round, no doubt to emphasise once and for all his absolute wish not to be followed, then tempered his severe expression with a smile, took his wife by the arm with a gesture of emancipation and disappeared. Herst felt his anxiety increase and his heart sink. He reproached himself for having acquiesced in what he could not help regarding as a serious breach of security. He should have protested more forcibly, raised further objections, threatened to hand in his resignation. Now it was too late.

He shrugged his shoulders. After all, he was conscious of having acted for the best, within the limits of the instructions and even slightly beyond them. He gave a few brief orders to one of the two men with him, the one who had stayed behind by the car. The other had already disappeared into the wood, taking a path that climbed up a steep slope leading away from the creek. Herst set off along the same path, which, after countless twists and turns, came out on to the summit of a tall peak, covered in brambles, overlooking the creek from a great height. It was an arduous climb, but he reached the top without too much panting. He was still in excellent physical shape. His man was there, on watch, with a carbine in his hand.

"Well?"

"They haven't arrived on the beach yet. I can only see the end of the road, which they haven't yet reached."

"Probably romping about on the way, like a couple of schoolchildren playing truant," Herst growled angrily.

"But I have a good view of the beach."

"Just as well. And they can't see you at all?"

"Impossible."

"Again, just as well," Herst muttered. "Just as well for me and for you. You realise what I mean?"

161

Even at the threat of a ruthless reprimand, even at the fear of offending his boss, Herst had not been able to decide to carry out his orders to the letter. His professional conscience had prevailed over his scruples. He was going to keep an eye on his President, come what may—an eye and a weapon ready to be used. The man chosen for this post was a first-class shot, even better than Herst himself, who was nevertheless a more than fair marksman. Granted, he was too far from the beach to be able to take action with any degree of efficacy, but his mere presence reassured him somewhat. As for himself, Herst, he was going to climb down again to the road, near his other assistant, but he had not been able to resist coming up here and personally inspecting the observation post.

He examined the beach, kneeling beside his subordinate.

"Deserted," the man muttered. "Not a bather in sight. Only a camper's tent among the pine-trees."

"I know who he is," Herst murmured. "Nothing to fear from him."

"I really don't think there's any danger."

Herst replied that he hoped not, in a grumpy tone which barely concealed the anguish that had assailed him since Pierre Malarche's disappearance round the bend in the road.

"There they are! They're coming down to the beach."

Herst felt immensely relieved. The mere fact of seeing the couple with his own eyes seemed a sort of security. This was why he had not been able to resist climbing up to the observation post.

The President and his wife were now by the edge of

162

the creek. They paused for a moment, not for the first time since their departure, and, after a casual glance at the camper's tent, which gave no sign of life, exchanged a long kiss on the lips. This demonstration of affection had the effect of suddenly exasperating Herst who was watching the scene through his binoculars. He was unable to repress an angry snort, flung his instrument down on the ground and felt an urge to fall flat himself among the brambles, as though in a fit of madness, to give full rein to his fury. His outburst lasted a good minute, during which he thumped the rock with his clenched fist, calling heaven and earth to witness the imbecile job he was obliged to do.

"What the hell are they up to now?" he enquired after he had recovered a little composure.

"They're undressing," his subordinate blithely announced. "They're in their bathing togs and . . ."

"Just as well," Herst snorted.

"I think they're going into the sea."

They exchanged these remarks half out loud, the couple being much too far away to overhear them. They themselves could not catch the words of endearment that were now being exchanged between husband and wife. They merely saw the young woman raise her arms to the sky with a gesture of deliverance, throw back her shoulders and inhale the sea air voluptuously, but could only guess at the sense of the words that accompanied these movements:

"Darling, I've been waiting for this moment for ages! Alone at last, just the two of us, with no one to bother us. Free at last!"

9

GAUR HAD NOT TAKEN HIS EYES OFF the couple from the moment he saw them appear at the edge of the creek, while they were still some distance from the sandy beach on which he was pinning so much hope. He too witnessed the long kiss they exchanged by the water's edge. He too saw the young woman disengage herself from her husband's embrace, slip out of her clothes in the twinkling of an eye and scamper down to the sea. It was not long before Pierre Malarche followed suit, and the various clandestine onlookers had the privilege of observing the spectacle of the Head of State in bathing trunks, playfully rushing off in pursuit of his young wife who was already swimming out to sea, both of them uttering childish cries of delight.

In the creek, which echoed to the sound of their frolics, the two of them amused themselves like children on holiday. Pierre Malarche had not felt so carefree for ages and the antics of his young wife made him burst out laughing the whole time. This day was all the more precious to him for its having been obtained by trickery and for his having had such difficulty in fitting it in among all his tedious official chores. He

164

was firmly resolved to make it last as long as possible. He had no urgent business to attend to today. The whole of France believed him to be in a country house several miles away. He would not in fact be going there until shortly before nightfall. And so they went on with their fun and games for a long time, swimming and diving off the sheer rocks into the crystal-clear water. It was only after exhausting all the pleasures of the sea that, out of breath, they finally decided to regain dry land, longing now for the heat of the sun.

They staggered slightly as they came out of the water, inspected the deserted stretch of beach and hesitated no longer than a second. With the merest nod of agreement, they made their way spontaneously towards the particularly enticing patch of sand, unsullied by twigs or driftwood and, at this hour of the day, lying out of the shade of the pine-trees. Here they spread out their bath towels and lay down side by side, without speaking, their faces raised towards the sky. Some dozens of yards behind them, Olga grasped her companion by the shoulder.

Martial Gaur knew that his hour had come. Until then he had undergone a lengthy ordeal divided between impatience, fear and a sort of regret. The impatience was due to their unexpectedly protracted bathe, during which the sun was shifting in the sky, changing the interplay of light and shadow. His fear was that Verveuil might get tired of waiting and attempt a long-range shot while they were still in the water, which, besides being risky, would not afford a spectacular picture even if it came off.

165

His regret was likewise of a professional kind. He felt he might be letting some rare opportunities slip through his fingers. A powerful instinct impelled him at every moment to focus his camera on the couple and register a few of the exceptional and valuable images that were now unfolding before his eyes. It was a series of temptations which he found difficult to resist, and he had moreover yielded to the first: the image of the Head of State and his young wife locked in each other's arms in a deserted creek! This picture alone was bound to cause a sensation. He had focused, then pressed the shutter release on the spur of the moment.

To refrain from repeating this incautious move, he had had to reason with himself, to take himself to task and remind himself of the amount of patience and ingenuity he had expended in preparing the creation of a matchless work of art. It was only by pondering on this masterpiece with all his will, by concentrating all the strength of his vision on the incomparable sparkle of this unique black diamond which eclipsed every other precious stone, that he managed to resist the temptation and continue to lie doggo in his lair. Even if there was little chance of his being spotted while taking a few snaps of them bathing, a vague sense of duty, a painful but sacred duty imposed by the supremacy of a sovereign art, forbade him to take the slightest risk.

His heart started beating at a frantic speed when he saw the bathers emerge from the water and make their way towards the spot he had chosen for them. God be praised! It was not too late. The interplay of light and shade was scarcely modified. The three rocks in the shape of an eagle were sparkling even more intensely than he had hoped.

He held his camera up to his eye. What on earth was Verveuil waiting for? Pierre Malarche had been lying motionless for over a minute. A film of sweat beaded the photographer's brow.

He calmed down as soon as he saw the barrel of a rifle protrude from the undergrowth between the two outcrops of granite, deflect slightly, traverse for a brief moment, then come to a standstill. It was once again with complete self-possession that he put his eye to the viewfinder, and held his finger poised on the shutter release.

Did his somewhat abrupt gesture make the tent and the surrounding pine-needles quiver? Or was a ray of sunshine reflected from his camera as he leant outside slightly? The fact was that Malarche's attention was attracted and he suddenly raised himself on one elbow, his face turned towards the tent, an expression of annoyance in his eyes, perturbed by the suspicion that his orders were not being carried out.

This sudden gesture saved him from having his brains blown out. The bullet aimed at his head struck him in the shoulder. Martial Gaur had taken his first exposure at the very moment of the shot. As he was operating for the second time, his infallible eye realised straight away that the President had not been killed. Pierre Malarche was lying flat on the ground, grasping his injured shoulder with his good hand. His face betrayed nothing but intense astonishment. There was no trace of the heart-rending expression which the photographer had hopefully envisaged.

167

A gust of panic made Martial's blood run cold: the fetid breath of failure. But he had no time to waste on cursing this stroke of fate. Herst and his men must already be rushing down to the beach. He himself hurried towards the victim in order to snap him at point-blank range according to plan, even if the President's reactions were not living up to his own hopes.

While he covered the course he had studied so carefully as fast as possible, being obliged nevertheless to keep one eye on the ground to avoid the obstacles, he had the impression, or rather a definite perception, that several important things were happening simultaneously in the creek.

To begin with, there was a second shot, just as he was coming out of his tent, so close upon the first as to sound like its echo. This did not surprise him at once; he was waiting, he was hoping with all his might, for another attempt from Verveuil to make up for his initial blunder. But the impression of an echo filled him with foreboding. A third detonation confirmed his suspicion that the shooting was coming from another direction. Immediately afterwards his ear registered the sound of branches snapping, of undergrowth being trampled down, as though by someone in headlong flight. Then, down on the beach itself, a shadow flitted across his path, running along the water's edge towards the road, while he still had his eyes on the ground. Finally, as he drew closer to the body lying on the sand, he noticed, this time distinctly, another figure emerging from the wood and racing towards the injured man.

His mind was working at a prodigious speed, even faster than his nimble fingers manipulating the controls on his camera while his eye registered a fresh image. It took him only a second to apprehend the new development in the drama, as he prepared for the next exposure.

The last two shots had been fired by the bodyguards who were no doubt observing the beach from some distant post. Maybe they had noticed the barrel of the rifle? More probably they had fired into the wood at random. And this had been enough to terrify Verveuil. This pantomime killer had cravenly taken to his heels. It was his headlong flight he could still hear in the bushes. "The dirty dog!" Gaur reflected. "I might have known it."

The shadow encountered on the beach was the President's wife. She was likewise running away, screaming for help. Once again he contemptuously reflected, "That's all that can be expected from a slut like that." All these sensations, reflections and even moral judgements fell into place in his brain with the speed of lightning, while with a sinking heart he prepared to focus his camera on a grotesque caricature of the splendid image he had been carefully working out for weeks.

But his disillusion was of short duration and he did not even have time to curse this stroke of fate. It had no doubt been decreed somewhere in heaven or on earth that Martial Gaur would today be subjected to exceptional ordeals, that he would undergo alternations of anguish and hope that were enough to break the strongest nerve.

Just when all seemed lost, at the very moment providence appeared to have abandoned him, the drama suddenly became fraught with fresh possibilities, with promises beyond even his wildest dreams.

10

OLGA WAS THE NEW CHARACTER who had appeared on the scene, Olga who, far from cravenly taking to her heels like Verveuil, was now rushing on the President like a fury, moved by a passion comparable to his own which, in his case, made the danger of bullets unworthy of consideration. Keeping his camera trained on the President, who was now in focus, Martial Gaur watched her out of the corner of his eye, his heart once again pounding with hope, for Olga held a long pointed knife in her hand.

"What a woman!" he reflected. "I didn't misjudge her at all." Never had he felt so close to her. He witnessed her assault with a feeling of immense desire, and with all his gratitude. She appeared to him at this moment like an angel come down from heaven to redeem the misdeeds of a miserable wretch. He still had time to mumble a desperate prayer: "May she be able to handle the weapon properly! May her hand not falter!" But the thought that she was a gangster's daughter spontaneously crossed his mind and at once reassured him. The daughter of Pierrot le Bourgeois

170

was bound to have inherited a number of atavistic reflexes, and her face expressed such fierce determination that his last fears were dispelled.

She had reached her victim in a few strides. The photographer pressed the shutter release at the very moment she raised her knife, then automatically pulled a lever to wind on the film.

An instinctive gesture of the President, who had his head turned in the direction of this fresh attack, saved him once again. With his good hand he parried Olga's blow. She stumbled, lost her balance and fell down beside him, while the knife slipped from her fingers and landed in the sand. She at once stretched out her hand to retrieve it, but Malarche had managed to seize her other arm and twist it behind her back, maintaining a firm grip on her, putting his last ounce of strength into this reflex of self-defence.

Thus paralysed, Olga kept reaching in vain for the weapon which lay only a yard away. Martial Gaur uttered an obscene oath. She would never be able to retrieve it. With his muscles contracted in semi-consciousness, Malarche would not release his hold before help arrived. Martial glanced over his shoulder and noticed Herst, followed by his men, barely fifty yards off.

He turned back to the group lying at his feet and paused for a moment in contemplation, as though hypnotised by the heart-rending picture formed by that suppliant hand groping for the knife. His trance was of short duration, but during it he was overwhelmed by a tumultuous succession of intense feelings unrelated to actual time, like those dreams which fizzle out after a fraction of a second but which evoke sufficient thoughts and subconscious sensations to fill several hours on end.

He had the impression of having reached, after a long and arduous climb, the top of a pass from which he was able to view and almost touch with the tip of his finger the dazzling peak of triumph, but the final slope leading to the ultimate conquest demanded a far greater effort from him than the relatively easy path he had followed up till then. The outcome of the drama was not as he had originally planned it. He had to re-draft it, re-create it, and at a moment's notice; for, on the razor's edge on which he was teetering, it needed a mere puff, a moment's hesitation, to send him plunging into the chasm lying open at his feet: the grisly pit of failure. And the final climb, the victory which was once again in sight, no longer depended on the puppets whose strings he had been manipulating from afar. It was not a question of inspiration or occult influences. The future of his masterpiece demanded personal action from him. Destiny had provided only an inert instrument, which he would have to bring to life. There it was, at his feet, a mere inch or two from his leg, that damned leg of his.

It was on the knife that his eyes rested during the infinitesimal time his trance lasted—time enough to conceive the birth and death of a universe.

The blade lying on the sand radiated the fiery glow of the Provençal sun, reflecting a shimmering cascade of fantastic images which found an echo in Martial

172

Gaur's inflamed brain, evoking a succession of out-landish analogies. The cutting edge of the knife appeared to him like the narrow ledge on which he had the impression of balancing precariously between a peak of glory and a pit of abjection, or like the arm of the hypersensitive scales which at this very moment was determining the chances of the final apotheosis.

It was the point of the blade especially that fascinated him. The point of the blade was emitting invisible rays a thousand times more intense even than the brightest sunbeams. The point at which the two cutting edges converged represented to his feverish mind the dazzling peak of triumph, the radiant pole of all his ambitions, which for years he had glimpsed in his dreams without ever being able to approach it in reality, a sort of mystical ultimate marking the total gratification of his desires, set in the heart of a paradise reserved for the audacious few. The weapon as a whole had assumed the sacred value of a symbol and become the flaming banner of an esoteric religion which the god of the privileged élite—an arrogant god, but a god who occasionally deigned to show interest in certain human reactions—had flung at his feet to measure his determination and test his valour.

A mere fraction of a second, an atom of time expanded by a prodigious mental struggle, exalted by a cyclone of passions sufficiently violent to last a lifetime! This paroxysm could not be prolonged with impunity and time was too precious to allow him further hesitation. This was one of those exceptional sets of circumstances when the artist has to make a snap decision, an instantaneous decision, as instantaneous as the pressing of a shutter release, as the blinking of an eyelid, the blinking of Olga's eyelids—those eyes whose burning gaze he felt directed on himself.

A strange sense of peace came over him. His mind was made up. Certain gestures, fraught with immense significance, are sometimes trivial. This was one of them. It was scarcely perceptible. It encroached only slightly on the dogma of impartiality by which the photographer still abided. Martial did not even have to bend down.

A slight nudge with the tip of his toe, a perfectly natural movement of his artificial leg, as though unconsciously kicking aside an obstructive pebble, sent the knife slithering forward within reach of Olga's hand.

The deed was done. All that remained for him was to step a few paces back, fling himself flat on the ground, raise his camera to his eye and take the sensational photograph he had been seeking all his life and which fulfilled at last his wildest dreams.

He pressed the shutter release for the first time just as the point of the knife pierced the President's breast. The expression of hatred engraved at this moment on Olga's face would of itself have justified the value of this picture.

He still had time to take a second exposure, just before Herst pounced on her—a point-blank view of the wretched President now mortally wounded, a photograph which fixed for eternity all the horror of the death agony, enhanced by a profusion of details which no camera operator had ever before assembled in one exposure, a unique document by virtue of the personality of the principal subject, the sumptuousness of the setting, to which the wounded eagle spreading its wings above the bloodstained body added a romantic touch, the final touch that was required to arouse feelings of frenzy in the general public at the same time as admiration among connoisseurs and artists—the unmistakable hallmark of success.